THE ANDERSON CHRONICLES
BOOK 3

JUSTICE RENDERED

KIT KARSON

Book design by Bookery.design

ISBN 979-8-9873287-8-1 (hard cover)
ISBN 979-8-9873287-9-8 (paperback)
ISBN 979-8-9900561-0-7 (ebook)
ISBN 979-8-9900561-1-4 (audiobook)

TO DARLENE, RONDA, AND SHIRLEY

Who add the polish

IF I WHET MY GLITTERING SWORD,
AND MY HAND TAKES HOLD ON JUDGEMENT,
I WILL RENDER VENGEANCE TO MY ENEMIES,
AND REPAY THOSE WHO HATE ME.

Deuteronomy 32:41

1

SHERIFF PETER ELLIOT sat high above town on his front porch swing, listening as the hum of vehicles and voices faded, replaced with breeze-rustled leaves and an occasional yipping dog. At times like these, in the deep quiet of the night, Peter would pause the creaking of his swing and listen closely. Echoes from a time gone by flowed from the accumulated dust of eroded granite that made up the rough earthen streets of Anderson, Montana. Muffled rattles of wagon wheels and cracking whips blended with neighing horses and the clang of a blacksmith's hammer. Such was life in the original settlement, an outpost of the vast Anderson Ranch. Among locals it was acknowledged that the small town of Anderson, deep in the center of Stone County, Montana, carried an unexplainable aura of enchantment.

Peter woke cold and stiff, the pattern of the porch swing cushion etched into his cheek and his mahogany hair more unruly than usual. A hot shower loosened his joints and a vigorous walk in the crisp morning air cleared the fog from his brain. Late summer rains rutted the dirt road leading from Peter's cozy bungalow to Anderson's stately brick and granite courthouse. Peter carefully traversed the rough road while his German Shepherd, Zack, trained police dog and faithful friend, jogged by his side, stopping now and then to sniff under a bush.

In the second-floor sheriff's department, Peter found his deputies gathered around a white bakery box, engaged in their morning ritual of donuts and updates.

Crumbs dusted Deputy Helen's uniform shirt and filtered through cracks between buttons and straining fabric. She kept her hair in a honey-highlighted bob rather than the long gray braid from past years but was losing the battle with her weight. Complacency brought on by contentment kept her dipping into the donut box.

"Huckleberries are ripe," she said. "I saved you a jelly-filled."

"Thanks," said Peter, pulling up a chair and picking the last huckleberry donut out of the box. He broke off a piece and tossed it to Zack. "Anything exciting happening?"

"It's quiet even for Anderson," replied Travis, blond and buff office clerk, and forensic enthusiast. "Not a single drunken fight or domestic call last night."

"Good. Where's Angus?"

"Out on a complaint. The perpetual garage sale is oozing onto the sidewalk again."

Peter rolled his eyes. "Does it seem to you he collects more stuff than he sells?"

"My theory is Fred ran out of room in his own house and bought an empty lot for expansion," said Helen.

"I'll go give Angus a hand." Peter grabbed a chocolate-frosted and whistled for Zack. "Fred could argue the teats off a milk cow."

"You forgot your hat," said Travis.

Peter found folks expected a western sheriff to dress the part, and responded accordingly. That and his six-foot-five, two-hundred-pound frame lent authority to his position. He lifted his required Stetson off the rack and tapped it firmly into place with only a minuscule smudge of chocolate on the brim.

The closest route to Main Street and the perpetual garage sale was through the hidden exit in Peter's office and that's the way he chose to go. In the late 1800s, when the courthouse was being built, the sitting sheriff made a special request for the secret doorway. He could think of no better way to avoid angry citizens and pesky reporters. Peter appreciated the shortcut. A brief walk down a steep hill and across the street brought him to the one blemish in an otherwise pretty place.

Angus's face was almost as red as his hair, his tightly wound wiry frame on the verge of erupting. Fred's enormous sweatpants-clad bottom was stuffed in a recliner in the middle of the boardwalk, and he remained unmoved as did the hodgepodge cluttered around him. An end table filled with empty pop cans and snack bags sat next to the chair.

"Hey, Fred," said Peter, aware of the relief on Angus's face at the sound of reinforcement.

"Sheriff. Good to see you. Are you looking for anything in particular? I'm holding back a few special items for exclusive customers."

"No, Fred. I'm not shopping. Do you have a license to hold a sidewalk sale?"

Fred scratched a large mole on his chin, pursed his thick lips, and considered. "Well, no, I don't believe I do."

With a wide-mouthed smirk, he pulled a folded sheet of paper, smudged and torn, from his faded plaid shirt pocket. Making a show of smoothing the wrinkles, clearing his throat, and flicking a long tongue, he read:

"City ordinance five-two dash four. Retail businesses are permitted to use the area in front of their stores in the process of conducting business." He folded the paper and returned it to his pocket.

"You're missing a few important points."

"And what would those be, Sheriff?"

"You know perfectly well you don't have a retail business license. You have a special 'garage sale' permit. Even if you did have the proper license, you would be in violation."

Fred's smug smirk visibly sagged.

"The ordinance states there must be at least five feet of walking space between displays of merchandise and the roadway. You've taken up the entire boardwalk. People are walking in the street to get around you and your mess."

Fred eyed a group of tourists giving him dirty looks as they stepped into the gutter. Few suspected decaying concrete sidewalks were hidden beneath the weathered wooden boardwalks, or that the colorful paint adorning late Victorian era houses dressed in towers and turrets was anything but original. Visitors came to immerse themselves in the romance of another era and Fred's overflowing lot of modern-day trash marred the illusion.

"If you continue reading the ordinance, you will also note that sale items may only be displayed between the hours of eight a.m. and five p.m. According to the complaint our office received, you've had your junk sitting out here night and day for an entire week."

Fred's large face puffed in irritation. "This is pure discrimination, Sheriff. I intend to file a harassment complaint."

"You can do that when you come to the courthouse to pay your fine. Write him a ticket, Angus."

Fred bristled. "A ticket for what!"

"Public nuisance. That's up to five hundred dollars and/or six months in jail. You'd better hope Judge Knowles is having a good day."

Angus flipped the cover on his ticket book, arranged the pages, and clicked open his pen. "How do you spell your last name, Fred?"

Fred crossed his arms and huffed.

"We could charge you with refusing to comply with a police officer," said Peter.

"F. I. L. M. O. R. E."

"Filmore?" clarified Angus, as he wrote the letters. "Yeah."

Angus finished filling out the ticket and laid it on the cluttered end table after Fred refused to take it.

"The ticket is valid whether you take it out of the officer's hand or not, Fred," said Peter.

He turned back as he and Angus were walking away. "We'll be back at five oh one. If this boardwalk isn't cleared, you'll get another citation."

2

I N T H E E A R L Y days, finding a job never crossed Fred's mind. He sponged off his mother until she died and her social security benefits departed with her. All she left him was a ramshackle farmhouse with a pleasant view. Food stores running low, Fred coveted a cash cow. An actual animal would be too much work and he had no intention of working for a living.

Flipping through television channels one day, Fred stumbled on *American Pickers,* a show about two men traveling the countryside, sorting through sheds and barns, looking for antiques and collectibles. Dumbfounded at first, he became intrigued at the worth of what some people would consider junk. He studied and took notes, watching several antique shows and reading antiquing magazines until he had a basic knowledge.

Fred realized he had an abundance of treasure in his mother's house. While he emptied the attic of cherished family heirlooms, he learned the trade and made connections with buyers. Eventually, he reached the bottom of his mother's hoard and was forced to hit the road in search of other people's treasures.

Deserted farmhouses and barns were Fred's top choice. Most were looted before he got there, but now and then he found a place locked and left vacant. The owners either dead or warehoused in an old folks home and the house left to rot.

Fred traded his sedan for a cargo van and invested in a tire iron for breaking windows and doors. He traveled in ever widening circles, robbing and looting as he went. As soon as he had the van full of potential treasures he left an area, leaving plenty of distance between the robbery and his next big heist.

Success brought confidence. In areas scarce of abandoned homesteads, he targeted those still inhabited, scouting places with a rundown air, folks in need of cash. Fred lacked natural charm and had never been taught manners, but he studied what he saw on television and mastered the art. He cleaned himself up. A haircut and neat button-down plaid shirt. Cowboy boots and a silver belt buckle from a pawn shop. He found it appealed to ranchers and their wives, made them feel at ease. He learned patience.

Fred perfected his scam through decades of practice. He was lazy, but he wasn't stupid. His cost of goods was zero and profits were high. A negative was the amount of work he had to put out in order to acquire goods. While ruminating over the problem in a diner one day, he overheard a conversation in the next booth. Two men discussed in hushed tones "cargo" and "acquisition" and, best of all, "antiques." To innocent ears, the conversation was between legitimate businessmen. Fred knew better. One look told him these were not businessmen. Grubby jeans, stained T-shirts, callused hands. These were looters. He picked up his plate and pushed his way uninvited into the booth and conversation. Undercover law enforcement couldn't be as convincing as Fred. The men readily confessed to pilfering and moving antiques and collectibles for another dealer. Fred offered them a better deal. Instantly he moved up in the hierarchy of stolen goods, from looter to dealer.

Solving one problem brought on another. He needed a permanent place to store stock, somewhere for his new looter employees to deliver goods. Somewhere remote, under the radar of law enforcement.

Fred studied a map of the United States, followed back roads to Interstate 90, and headed west. As he drove, cities became smaller and further apart.

Abandoned homesteads dotted the landscape. Rugged mountains loomed in the distance.

Late one night, in search of a motel, Fred exited the interstate, took a wrong turn, and found himself on a two-lane highway. Too tired to turn around, he decided to drive to the nearest town.

The sign along the road read, 'Welcome to Anderson Montana.' Good enough. A red neon 'vacancy' caught his eye. 'The Sapphire Inn' held steady in blue. Even in the dark he could see the motel had seen better days. It would do for the night. He would get himself back on track in the light of day.

3

PETER WATCHED HIS desk clock flip to five p.m. He stuck a paperclip in his paperback to hold the place and tucked it into his desk drawer.

Angus poked his head in the door.

"Ready to check on Fred?"

"Grab your citation pad. There's no way he moved all that stuff off the boardwalk by himself."

"How did he get it out there?"

"Good point. We can always hope."

Peter left his hat on the hook. There are certain things a Stetson can't fix. He whistled to Zack. "Let's get this over with."

Angus, Zack, and Peter took the shortcut through his narrow office stairway and down the steep dirt hill. Holly Noelle, owner of The Sapphire Pit, where tourists sifted through buckets of dirt in search of sapphires, was standing on the boardwalk in front of her sorting lot, staring across the street.

"Hi, Holly," said Peter, remembering the days when that 'hi' would have been followed by a hug and a kiss.

Holly brushed an errant strand of dark curls out of her eyes, leaving a smear of dirt on her forehead. "Look what he did," she said, pointing across the street.

If Peter were a betting man, he'd say the mound had grown since the confrontation that morning, or maybe it was the added décor. Twinkling Christmas lights wrapped around tattered lamp shades and snaked through twisted metal bed frames. Dozens of balloons floated on colorful metallic cords tied to various pieces of junk.

"I guess that's our answer," said Angus.

Holly gave Peter an accusing look. "What did you do to cause this reaction?"

"He's hardly a victim. I told him to get his junk off the boardwalk."

Peter stepped off the curb and crossed the street, Zack at his side. The battered easy chair was empty of everything except a thick layer of potato chip crumbs.

"Fred!" yelled Peter into the jungle of second-hand treasures.

No answer.

"You take that side, Angus, and I'll go around the other. He has to be in there somewhere."

Peter glanced to the side and then across the street. Angus, attention entirely focused on Holly, jumped when Peter yelled, "Angus!"

A deep red blush covered his freckles as he trotted across the street. Flirting with the boss's ex-girlfriend wouldn't earn him any brownie points.

"Fred has to be in this mess somewhere," repeated Peter. "You go around that way and I'll search in this direction."

An odor of decay and mold permeated the inner sanctum of the perpetual garage sale. Angus gagged, pulled a silk scarf out of a pouch on his duty belt, and wrapped it around his face. Peter contemplated his chances of a lung infection. They searched through wobbly stacks of cast-off furniture and racks of used clothes until they met in the middle.

"Looks like he decorated and then hightailed it out of here," said Angus. "Do you know where he lives?"

"In an old farmhouse next to the landfill, last I knew. That's where he gets most of this stuff."

Avoiding the awkwardness of Holly across the street, Peter led Angus up the hill to the historic Clara Hotel, built by town founder Charles Anderson for his wayward daughter. A man of honor, Charles lived and died unaware that Clara ran a lucrative brothel in the elegant hotel.

A dapper man in a coat and vest reminiscent of the style worn in the old west stood at the hotel entrance. Manager Phil Meyer, hands on hips and a scowl on his face, confronted Peter. "You've got to do something about that mess, Sheriff. On top of the unsightly view, when the wind gets up just right, the smell goes straight into our dining room. If it's blowing hard enough, the stench clears out the guest rooms upstairs. We've had three reservations walk out today."

"We're working on it, Phil. Are you the one who called in the complaint?"

Phil looked worried. "This is all confidential, isn't it?"

"Fred's mess on the boardwalk is against city ordinance. It's not like you don't have anything to complain about."

"Don't want to start any trouble though," said Phil with a nervous laugh, backing away a few steps. "You won't tell Fred I said anything, will you?"

"Not if he doesn't ask. You have a good day, Phil." Peter whistled to Zack and continued his hike up the hill, Angus close at his heels.

"That was weird," said Angus. "Almost like he's afraid of Fred."

"Yeah. Weird. Let's go find Fred."

In the courthouse parking lot, Peter opened the side door of his Ford Explorer and loaded Zack into the special canine kennel compartment. He and Angus climbed in the front and buckled their seat belts. They drove through town, shaking their heads at the now decorated eyesore of Fred's lot.

The county landfill was located south of town, strategically far enough in the hills to prevent runoff contamination of Flint Creek and secluded enough to keep debris and odor from reaching town or outlying farmsteads. Outside the gates of the landfill, a pot-holed dirt track led into a shallow ravine and around to the back of the main dumping area.

The Explorer bounced its way along the rough track, tossing Angus and Peter against the windows and straining seatbelts. Zack was reduced to whimpers and Angus held his hands out to protect his face and head from the beating.

"Are you sure this is a road?" he asked.

As they neared the lowest part of the ravine, Angus was surprised to see that only the front of the landfill was enclosed. The tall chain link fence ended abruptly at the bottom of the pit.

"What's the point of the gate in front?" asked Angus, a recent transplant from the nearby town of Rumsey.

"The town council didn't want to spend the money to fence the entire area. They figured most people would stop at a locked gate and not bother to drive around back."

"I agree. Not many people would brave this road."

The turbulence came to an abrupt end in front of a decrepit clapboard farmhouse decades past its prime. White paint, now faded and cracked, exposed aged pine boards turned to gray. Sagging porch steps and cardboard-covered windows blended into a background of discarded appliances and rusting farm equipment.

"Is this part of the landfill?"

"Nope. Welcome to 'Maison de Fred'."

"He lives here?"

"Last I knew."

A battered 1970s-era orange and white Chevy pickup sat parked in the shell of a decaying garage.

"Is that his truck?" asked Angus.

Peter shrugged and opened his door. He stepped out and let Zack out of his kennel. "Stay close, Zack. There's too much junk for you to be running around."

Angus followed Peter up the porch steps to the front door. As Peter knocked, the door swung open.

"Fred," Peter called. "It's Sheriff Elliott." He could see through the opening that the house was dark. A lack of noise or movement hinted that the house was empty.

"He could be lying in there dead," observed Angus. "Sufficient reason for us to enter."

Peter pushed the door open further and they stepped into clutter and filth. Angus gagged, pulled his silk scarf out of its pouch, and wrapped it around his mouth and nose. "It smells like something died in here."

"I need to get one of those scarves," said Peter, plugging his nose and covering his mouth with his hand.

The front door opened into a living room. Stacks of rubble lined the walls. Threadbare carpet of an indiscernible color covered what could be seen of the floor. Beer cans and pizza boxes were scattered across a shabby couch. A stained and sagging recliner faced a shiny new large screen TV.

"That's interesting," said Peter.

"Stolen?"

"A possibility but remember the number one rule."

"I know. I know. Never assume."

A doorway led to the kitchen. Food wrappers, tin cans, and a thick layer of grime covered faded and cracked linoleum. Paper plates coated with remnants of rotting food filled the sink.

"That explains the smell."

Peter and Angus stepped gingerly around hundreds of magazines escaping stacks on stairs leading to the second floor. An inspection of two upstairs rooms revealed much of the same. The treasures of a hoarder filled the first room from floor to ceiling and into the doorway. The next room, a bedroom, reeked of sour sweat and dirty socks. The imprint of an obese body was outlined in brown, stained sheets covering a sagging mattress. What they didn't find was Fred.

"Anything in the closet?" asked Peter.

Angus waded through piles of cast-off clothing and opened the door. "Just more clothes piled on the floor." He turned and looked at Peter. "No bodies."

"Maybe he's wandering around the landfill looking for treasures."

Search complete and eager for fresh air, Peter and Angus hurried down the stairs. They went through the open front door, carefully closing it behind them, and stood on the porch breathing deeply.

Peter pointed toward a well-worn path leading from Fred's house to the back of the landfill. "Let's take a look."

Not unlike the rest of Fred's life, trash oozed well past set boundaries. Roads wound around mounds of compost and recyclables. A bulldozer sat idle by a partially filled garbage pit, waiting for the county landfill operator to scrape and fill and cover. Magpies perched on high points, sunning themselves and hunting mice. Other than birds and rodents, the landfill was empty.

"What's the plan?" asked Angus.

"We'll drive back to town and check out Fred's lot on the off chance he cleaned it while we've been gone."

Zack had to be convinced to get into his kennel compartment after the rough ride to Fred's house. Peter relented and let him run to the main road.

"I'm tempted to run myself," said Angus, preparing for a beating.

⬥⬥⬥

BACK IN TOWN, Peter wasn't surprised to find the lot as they had left it, balloons and all.

"The lights will look pretty in the dark when you can't see the junk," commented Angus.

"Ha ha. Write the second ticket and mail it return receipt so he can't claim he didn't get it."

Peter parked in front of the lot. While Angus wrote out a ticket, Peter grabbed a roll of bright yellow crime scene tape out of the console and stepped into a crowd of spectators.

"What's the occasion, Sheriff?" asked one. "Why the lights and balloons?"

"Someone's idea of a joke," said Peter. He pushed his way through the crowd and strung tape from one corner of Fred's overflow to the other. By the time he was through, the crowd had lost interest and wandered to the other side of the street. He got into the Explorer and called the city office. Everyone was gone for the day, so he left a message requesting a special trash collection for the next morning.

Peter dropped Angus off at his vehicle and drove to the brewery. Some days called for a pizza.

4

SEVERAL YEARS EARLIER, after his night at The Sapphire Inn, Fred drove into town in search of breakfast. He studied the typical mishmash of buildings lining the street, Main Street according to the sign. Original miners' log cabins stood next to shabby nineteenth century brick homes. Decaying barns teetered into crumbling foundations. An appealing area for a looter. He smiled to himself. That wrong turn would pay off after all.

Rounding a curve in the road, Fred stopped in surprise. Cars lined both sides of the street and sidewalks teemed with people. Rather than decay, the buildings in this section of town spoke of prosperity.

A holiday? he thought as he studied the crowd. He tried to recall the date. Too late for Labor Day and too early for Thanksgiving. *Better yet.* Tourists.

A honking horn brought Fred back from his contemplations. Breakfast forgotten, he pulled into the first empty parking space he found and got out to explore.

The town stair-stepped into the foothills of a snow-dusted mountain. To the south, ski runs etched another slope. Rather than beauty, Fred saw opportunity. He studied the license plates of cars lining the street. Several came from an assortment of Montana counties, but just as many hailed from other states. This place was a tourist destination and tourists meant money. The variety of shops confirmed his suspicions. High-end local artisans, a candy store, souvenir T-shirts, and ice cream. And, most importantly, antiques.

5

STINKY AND SKINNY were odd companions for Nancy May, with her perfectly coifed wig and stylish clothes. Nancy, on the rare occasions she felt inclined to brag, would challenge anyone in town to compete with her wardrobe. But the wardrobe was a superficial pride and Nancy was not at heart a superficial person. She leaned toward eccentricity and was prone to boredom. Happiness came from surrounding herself with interesting people, no matter their hygiene status. And that is how she found herself one sunny summer afternoon at the county landfill, hunting discarded treasure.

Stinky was the secret name she used in her head. He called himself Roy, although Nancy had her doubts that was his legal name. Perpetually clad in extra-large Wrangler jeans, pointed-toed boots, and a straw hat, Roy fancied himself a cowboy. As Nancy watched him reach around his enormous gut to inspect a roll of wire, she had two thoughts: pity for the horse who had to haul him around, and he definitely needed longer arms.

"We've got copper here, Carl," said Stinky to Skinny.

Skinny Carl let out a hoot. "Y'see, Nancy, most metal can be turned in for cash. Copper's one of the best."

"Wonderful!" exclaimed Nancy, with feigned enthusiasm. She was more interested in a different type of treasure.

Nancy attended two separate weekly Bible studies at the Baptist church. Tuesday morning class was solemn and contemplative. Ruth Cook, oldest member of the congregation and spinster daughter of a pastor, led her group with discipline and authority. Homework was required and graded.

Linda Elliott, wife of Pastor Paul and sister-in-law to Sheriff Peter Elliot, led the Wednesday afternoon class. Emphasis was placed on joy and cookies and fellowship. In that group, Nancy had learned about the recent death of a local elderly man. After his death, the man's children cleaned out his house, hauled his possessions to the landfill, and put the house up for sale.

"He had beautiful antiques and collectibles," said Linda. "And there they were, smashed and broken in the landfill."

Nancy gasped in horror. "What a couple of nitwits... uh, I mean, didn't they know the value?"

"A son and a daughter, both spoiled and wealthy. I don't think they cared about the money. It was easier to throw everything away than sort it out."

"Those things could have been donated to charity."

"Too much bother. They didn't even have a funeral. Poor man."

The conversation drifted from there to the practice of visiting the landfill after funerals in search of overlooked family heirlooms. Several women sheepishly admitted to participating in those treasure hunts.

Returning to her apartment, Nancy stood at her kitchen window and watched Stinky and Skinny sorting odds and ends on a folding table set up on the narrow patch of grass between their building and hers. Scuttlebutt among fellow apartment dwellers was that the pair supplemented their disability income by scouring the local landfill for recyclable metals and turning them in for cash.

Nancy straightened the brim of her straw hat, smoothed her skirt, and marched purposely down the stairs and out to the sorting table.

"Howdy, Nancy May," said Roy in greeting.

"How often do you go to the landfill?"

"Almost every day when the weather's good," said Skinny Carl, straightening a handful of wire scraps. "This is the time of year folks clean out sheds and garages."

"And lots of construction," said Roy. "They throw away tons of stuff from remodels." He picked up a long copper pipe. "This is where the good money is."

"Oooh, that sounds like fun. I want to go with you," declared Nancy.

Stinky glanced at Skinny. Neither wanted to split their haul with a third person.

"I'm not interested in your pipes and wire," said Nancy, noticing the look. "I'm looking for antiques."

"Uh... sure. Okay. Meet us out front tomorrow after lunch."

And here she was, chiffon skirt billowing in the breeze and hat threatening to sail.

While Skinny Carl and Stinky Roy rummaged through discarded construction materials, Nancy walked the perimeter of the landfill searching for residential trash. Her sandals, although low heeled, prevented her from wading deeper into the layers of rubbish. She walked until she could go no further and, disappointed in not finding a treasure of her own, turned and made her way back toward the men. Before the construction dump, on the edge of the embankment, Nancy spotted a familiar bright blue disk. "I see a plastic kiddie pool," she called and pointed.

Carl set the brass fittings he was studying on top of his treasure pile and gingerly climbed over other discarded material until he was at the pool. "It sure is. I don't see a crack or anything. Do you want it?"

"Can you get it in the truck?" asked Nancy, pleased she had found a treasure. "I could use that to cover my garden this winter."

"Sure." He lifted the pool, flipped it right-side-up, and groaned. "People! They know grass clippings are supposed to go into the compost pile!"

Wet grass and hedge trimmings held the shape of the pool. Roy came over for a look and gave the clippings a kick with his pointed boot, causing the edges of the grass mold to crumble.

"What's that?" asked Carl.

Nancy leaned in closer, eyes straining to make out the odd shape beneath the grass. Two bulging eyes stared back. Connected to the eyes was a large green lump.

⁕

"HEY, BOSS," SAID Travis, poking his head into Peter's office. "Nancy May just called. The connection wasn't very good, but she said something about finding a giant toad at the landfill and you should come right away."

Peter grinned. Nancy May could spice up any dull day. "A giant toad?""

"That's what she said."

Peter stood and whistled to Zack. "Call Rick Jones at animal control and tell him to meet us at the landfill."

Travis chuckled. "He'll be thrilled to hear Nancy May's involved. He hasn't forgiven her for the skunk incident."

Although Travis wore the uniform well, he learned early on he didn't have the temperament to be a deputy. At times like these, he regretted being left behind.

***

ARRIVING AT THE landfill, Peter pulled inside the gates and found Nancy standing with two men, one skeletal thin and the other mimicking a quadruplet pregnancy. All three were staring into the garbage pit. Only Nancy glanced away briefly to acknowledge Peter.

Out of the vehicle, Zack stayed close to Peter's side as they approached the embankment. "Hello, Nancy. You called about a giant toad?"

Nancy pointed into the garbage pit toward a mound of grass clippings.

Peter had to admit the mound did resemble a giant toad, especially when he looked closer and found a pair of bugged eyes staring back at him. "Did any of you go down there?"

"I did," said Carl. "And Roy. We were gonna to bring the pool up for Nancy. That's when we found the toad."

"I've never in my whole lived life seen a toad that big," said the larger man, his open mouth revealing several missing teeth. "And I came from New Mexico. Those giant toads down there have bad juju. Touch their skin and your brain goes wonkers." He twirled his pointer finger around one temple. "No way I'm goin' near that one."

"Has it moved since you've been here?" asked Peter. Three nos and head shakes.

"Stay, Zack!" said Peter, preparing to climb into the pit. He contemplated toad juju and pulled a pair of gloves out of his duty belt.

"Who're your friends, Nancy?"

"St... I mean, Roy," she said, pointing at the larger man. "And Carl. They live in the apartment building next to mine."

"What are you doing out here?"

"They're teaching me about dumpster diving. It's all the rage, you know," she said, standing straighter and attempting an air of dignity.

"Sure." He slid down the embankment, slowing his descent with random roots growing through the dirt wall.

At the bottom, Peter leaned toward the green mound and bulging eyeballs. On closer inspection, he could see what he already suspected, the eyes were human and vaguely familiar. The grass clippings were damp and finely mulched, causing them to cling in a thick layer to the body hidden underneath. Peter pulled out his cell phone and punched in Travis's desk number.

"Yeah, Boss. Find a toad?"

"No, but I found a dead human body."

"No kidding?"

"No kidding. Where's Helen?"

"Out on patrol. Nothing going on though."

"Send her this way with her crime scene kit. Have Angus come too. He can help question Nancy and her friends."

"On it, Boss."

Peter looked up to find Rick Jones, Stone County animal control officer, standing next to the dumpster diving team, all staring down in shock.

"A dead body?" exclaimed Nancy. "A human body? Who is it?"

Peter leaned over with his gloved hand and gently brushed a layer of grass away from the swollen face. Fred of the perpetual garage sale.

6

"WHY IS HE naked?" asked Helen, after brushing several layers of grass from the body.

Sure enough. Underneath his grass blanket, Fred was naked to his toes.

"What's that sticking out of his head?" yelled Nancy, watching from above.

Peter bent and examined a silver shaft, covered in dried blood, protruding from Fred's left temple. A short section of three tines could be seen outside the skin. "It's a giant fork."

"A serving fork," observed Nancy. "He looks like a toad. Maybe someone was trying to eat him."

The four onlookers laughed hysterically.

"I said you could go home, Nancy," said Angus.

"I'm waiting for my swimming pool to be released. Besides, this is more interesting than anything going on at home."

"It's evidence in a crime. You'll have to find a pool somewhere else," Angus replied to her. "That's not just any fork," he said to Peter.

"What do you mean?"

"It looks like antique silver."

Peter looked at him, surprised. "How do you know that?"

"My mom collects antiques. She's really into silverware. I've learned a few things listening to her chatter about it over the years."

"Good to know," said Peter, turning back to the body. "And unless we have suicide by fork, this is murder." He pulled his phone out and punched in the number for Dr. Hamm.

"Hello, Peter. What's up?"

"We have a body. Looks like murder. We'll send him over for autopsy as soon as we finish working the crime scene."

"The clinic is slow today so perfect timing. I haven't had a good autopsy in a while."

"Uh... okay. I'll keep you posted." Sometimes Dr. Hamm was a little too enthusiastic about murder.

The crew took samples and measurements and pictures until the scene was thoroughly examined and cataloged.

"How're we going to get this pool back to the evidence room without too much contamination?" asked Helen, as they prepared to go.

"I can haul it in my pickup truck," said Roy, excited to be part of an investigation.

Helen looked at Peter. He shrugged "Why not?"

"I guess we could wrap it in plastic first."

"Would a tarp work?"

"Sure, if we tape it tightly."

"Good. I just happen to have a new tarp and a roll of duct tape in my Explorer. You never know when you'll have to wrap up a swimming pool."

Peter climbed the embankment to fetch the items as the Stone County ambulance rolled through the landfill gates driven by Dr. Hamm. He braked next to Peter and opened his window. In his mid-sixties, silver-haired and handsome, Dr. Hamm had more energy than many people much younger. "The ambulance crew was on a transfer to Missoula, so I came over myself."

"Thanks, Doc. You're too late to save this one, but you can help us figure out what killed him."

Dr. Hamm waited while Peter retrieved the tarp and tape from his vehicle, and they carried the ambulance gurney down the hill.

"Do you think the fork in his temple is the murder weapon, Doc?" asked Helen.

"Very likely. I won't know until I do the autopsy, but if he wasn't dead before that, a fork in the temple would finish the job."

It took the whole crew to lift Fred the Toad onto the gurney and carry him up the embankment to the ambulance.

"I need to lose weight before I die," muttered Helen. "This is undignified."

"The naked issue doesn't help," said Angus.

"Good point. I want to die skinny and dressed... and have my hair done."

Helen supervised the wrapping and taping of the swimming pool, making sure it was protected from contamination. Roy and Skinny Carl used bungee cords to secure it in the back of Roy's truck while Helen loaded grass samples, and other crime scene paraphernalia into her vehicle.

Dr. Hamm led the parade back to town in the ambulance, turning on the lights periodically to give ranch kids a show.

Last to leave the scene, Peter stopped outside the landfill gates and eyed the rough road to Fred's house. "Hang on, Zack," he said and began the bumpy ride down the hill.

The last time Peter was in Fred's house, he was looking for Fred. This time it was a possible crime scene. He parked at a distance and studied the area around the house. A heavy rain had fallen the night before, explaining why the grass clippings covering Fred were wet. Depending on when Fred was murdered, the rain could work in favor of an investigation. He lowered Zack's window to give him ventilation and said, "Stay, Zack."

Wild grasses and dirt surrounded the house. Peter opened his door and studied the ground beneath his feet. Still wet from the rain, it showed no signs of shoe or tire prints. He walked toward the front porch, carefully watching where he stepped and stopping periodically to look for disturbance in the mud. Finding none, he climbed the porch steps and let himself into the house, this time looking for evidence of an altercation.

Searching for disarray in the house of a hoarder took an illogical dose of optimism. Chairs were not overturned, trails of blood weren't trickling downstairs, or in this case, a silverware drawer full of priceless antiques wasn't turned over on the floor. Peter opened drawers in the kitchen. Fred's utensils were of the bargain bin variety. Contemplating the nakedness of the body, Peter thought back on his encounter with Fred the day before. In his mind, he could see Fred taking paper out of the pocket of a red and brown plaid shirt, huge navy-blue sweatpants filling the easy chair. Peter waded through stacks of magazines to the second floor and found the bathroom. A variety of clothes items were scattered on the floor, but not the plaid shirt and sweatpants. Towels on the floor, hooks, and towel bars were dry, showing no sign that Fred had taken a bath or shower recently. The soap bar in the bathtub was dry and cracked.

Peter moved on to the bedroom. There was no sign of the plaid shirt or sweatpants on top of any clothes piles or under the bed. The bed sheets were dirty, but devoid of obvious blood stains. Fred hadn't been murdered in his bed. Logistically, if he had died in his house, it would have taken several people to carry him out. Even then, they most likely would have dumped him in the rear of the landfill, closer to the house.

Exiting through the front door, Peter stood on the porch and surveyed the area. Fred didn't have a lawn. The grass clippings covering his body came from somewhere else. Peter walked down the steps, around the side of the house to the shell of a garage. There were no tracks in the mud. If the old pickup was Fred's mode of transportation, it hadn't moved since before last night's rainstorm. The truck was unlocked and as messy as the house. A quick search revealed no obvious blood stains. Fred wasn't killed in his truck.

Decaying cardboard boxes, discarded paint cans, and rusty garden tools cluttered the area. An enclosed utility trailer was parked between the house and garage. Peter pulled the doors open to find an assortment of scavenged items from the landfill.

He walked back to his Explorer and tossed Zack a doggie treat as an apology before letting him out to run to the main road. On the way to town, Peter called the sheriff's office.

"Hey, Boss," said Travis, picking up his desk phone.

"I'm on my way back to town. Anything going on?"

"Not much. We finally convinced Nancy and her buddies there was no need to deputize them. I bribed Roy and Carl with donuts. Nancy was a little harder."

Peter rolled his eyes. "Did Doc say when he would be finished with the autopsy?"

"He got called back to the hospital for an emergency. He said he'd get to it when he could."

Sigh. "Okay. Keep me posted. I'm going over to Paul and Linda's."

Peter drove to the Baptist church and parsonage where his older brother Paul and wife Linda Elliott lived, preached, and served their flock. Built with inheritance from the death of their parents, the parsonage sat in a pretty meadow above Flint Creek on the outskirts of town. The home was built in generous proportions, with a wrap-around porch and windows to match, a sanctuary in any season. During the warmer months, Paul and Linda moved folding tables onto the porch, side-by-side, where Paul studied and wrote his sermons and Linda wrote mystery books. Peter found them there, engaged in more relaxing than working. He let Zack out to chase squirrels and made his way to the porch.

"Did you come for dinner, Peter?" asked Linda in greeting.

"I wouldn't say no to a burger and a Cold Smoke." Paul yawned and stretched.

"Stay where you are," said Peter. "I'll start the barbeque."

Linda and Paul were Peter's secret sounding board when he had tough cases. Linda had a knack for solving mysteries. During dinner he filled them in on his newest investigation.

Occasionally, Paul would come up with a unique idea. "There's a lot of rage involved in stabbing someone in the head with a fork," he observed. "Follow the anger."

7

"**D**OC LEFT A message for you to call him," said Travis when Peter arrived at the office the next morning.

"Great! He must be done with the autopsy." Peter settled into his comfy leather chair, a gift from a grateful citizen, and picked up his desk phone.

"What do you have for me, Doc?"

"Other than obvious medical issues caused by obesity, poor diet, and a sedentary lifestyle, your victim would still be alive except for the large fork jammed into his brain."

"So, the fork was the cause of death?"

"No doubt. There was enough force behind that fork to fracture the skull. The fork and bone fragments from the fracture tore the middle meningeal artery. The tear was quite significant. Bleeding from the wound collecting in the brain caused an epidural hematoma and led to excessive pressure on the brain. He would have lost consciousness and eventually died.”

“Any other injuries?”

“No defensive wounds if that’s what you mean. The fork went in at an angle that suggests the attacker came at him from above. My guess is he didn’t see it coming.”

“So, he was either sitting and the attacker was standing over him, or he was standing, and the attacker was taller than Fred.”

“That about sums it up. He did have fresh scrapes on his hands and knees.”

“From before or after death?”

“Probably right around the time of death or shortly thereafter. There was bleeding, but no sign of healing.”

“Any idea what caused the scrapes?”

“There was a trace of oily dirt in the wounds.”

“Oily dirt?”

“Like from machinery.”

“Ah.”

“The lividity was interesting.”

“Remind me what lividity means.”

“When someone dies and the heart stops, blood stops flowing. Gravity causes the blood to settle into the lowest area of the corpse. The result is purplish-blue patches on the skin. The front of Fred's body and left side of his face, have lividity and a diamond pattern of blanching."

"Blanching?"

"When the weight of the corpse is pressing against the ground or some other hard object, the blood vessels are compressed and keep blood from pooling. The skin remains white rather than turning the purplish-blue of lividity."

"He was found on his back in the landfill. Was there any lividity or blanching on his back?"

"None. That tells me he was stabbed somewhere else, died in a prone position—face down—and was moved to the landfill. Lividity and blanching are permanent after about twelve hours. He lay wherever he died for that long before he was moved."

"Any ideas what caused the diamond pattern?"

"No. Nothing comes to mind. On another note, usually areas of clothing folds or seams, that sort of thing, will show in lividity. He had none of that."

"He tended to wear sweats and loose shirts, nothing that would bind."

"Even then the seams would show if the body was lying on them. My guess is he was naked at death or soon afterward."

"Estimated time of death?"

"The body was found around one thirty yesterday afternoon. Body temperature was seventy-five degrees, the same as outside air. Estimating time of death by temperature is unreliable if we don't know where a body has been and in what conditions. Cold rain would accelerate body cooling. I bring it up because it took some doing to wash that wet grass off him and he only had it on his front. It seems likely he was dumped during the rain and then the grass thrown on top."

"And then the pool on top of that, not to keep him dry, but to hide the body."

"Makes sense. As far as time of death, when his body was found, it was in full rigor mortis and lividity was fixed. I'm estimating death between sixteen and twenty-four hours before the body was found, which would be between one thirty and nine thirty in the evening the day before."

"We were writing him a ticket earlier that morning and he had the lot decorated with lights and balloons by five. That would have taken him a couple hours. Everything fits the time frame. Thanks, Doc. Oh, and Doc?"

"Yeah?"

"Save the fork."

"Already in an evidence bag, blood and tissues still attached."

"Thanks." Peter disconnected, leaned back in his chair, and contemplated the new information. "Travis," he called into the outer office. "When did the rain start on Tuesday night?"

He heard Travis's keyboard clicking as he looked up weather information. "Around one in the morning."

So where was the body between the time he was murdered until he was dumped? thought Peter. Lying face down on something with a diamond pattern, according to Doc.

"Did you have any luck tracing Fred's next of kin?"

Travis came to the door of Peter's office and leaned against the frame. "I've looked through all the usual databases and can't find anything."

Peter tapped his pen against his desk in thought. "So, nobody around here we need to notify."

"Nope."

"Okay. I'll send someone over to his house later. They might be able to find something in that mess. Where is everyone?" Peter asked.

"Helen's on traffic duty and Angus is on a trespassing call."

Peter stood and lifted his Stetson off its hook. "I guess I'm on murder investigation duty." He whistled to Zack and left by his back stairway.

Standing at the top of the steep hill gave Peter an eagle's eye view of Main Street and a perfect position to study the layout and plan his investigative questioning. He had already talked to Phil Meyers, the hotel manager, but there were more questions that needed asking.

Peter crossed the street, Zack at his heels, and walked as far as the Clara Hotel. Phil wasn't at his usual post in front, so Peter pushed through the old-fashioned brass revolving door. Phil stood at the front desk, lecturing a young clerk about telephone etiquette. A wary look crossed his face when he caught sight of Peter.

"Morning, Sheriff. Looking for a room?"

"No, thanks, I have a home, no need for a hotel room." He leaned on the counter and tipped his hat to the young clerk. "I do need to ask you a few questions, though."

"Ask away."

"We should go into your office."

"Uh, sure." Phil led Peter around the counter and down a short hallway. The office was small and cluttered. Phil moved a stack of ledger books from a chair in front of his desk and set them on the floor. "Have a seat."

Peter sat and removed his hat. Avoiding the clutter, Zack sat in the doorway. Phil squeezed around the desk and settled into his own battered office chair. "I hope this is about cleaning up that mess next door."

"When was the last time you saw Fred?" asked Peter.

Phil rubbed his chin. "Not today. I guess I haven't seen him since he was putting up those ridiculous balloons and lights. Was that yesterday? Nope. The day before. Tuesday."

"Did you talk to him?"

"No. I avoid talking to Fred. Confronting him about his mess encourages his bad behavior and I have no reason to chat with him about anything else."

"Do you remember the time of day when you saw him on Tuesday?"

Phil thought again. "It was around noon. Before the lights and balloons were up. I was on my way home for lunch. What's this all about, Sheriff? Is Fred missing?"

"Fred is dead. We believe he was murdered."

"What?! Who would murder Fred?"

"You didn't like him. In fact, you were upset about his mess oozing onto the boardwalk and the smell driving away business."

"I didn't dislike him enough to kill him. I expected the town council to make him clean up the mess. I thought that's what you came by to talk about."

"Can you think of anything unusual going on that day? Any strangers in the area?"

"There are strangers on the street every day, Sheriff, but I didn't notice anyone other than the typical tourist crowd."

"Where were you between the time you left here and early Wednesday morning?"

Phil looked shocked. "Am I a suspect?"

"Everyone's a suspect until we solve the crime."

Phil rubbed his chin again. "I left here just after five and went home. Spent the evening watching television. The usual."

"Can anyone confirm that you were home all night?"

"My wife, Pam."

"Okay, thanks, Phil," said Peter, getting up to leave. "Let me know if you remember anything else."

⁂

ELEANOR'S TEA PARLOR occupied the building on the other side of Fred's lot. Besides light sandwiches, baked goods, and tea, Eleanor sold greeting cards and upscale writing utensils. New and used books filled one back room and various local artisans displayed in another. More of a lady's shop, Peter had never had a reason to enter the store. As he reached to open the door, he spotted a sign taped to the glass:

Closed Today
Women's Club Luncheon
Community Center
12:00 – 2:00
Eleanor

Peter glanced at his watch. Noon thirty. The community center sat a block down and a street over from Eleanor's. She had only been in the community a few years, but her reputation as a caterer was firmly established. As Peter contemplated the appropriateness of a male at the Women's Club luncheon, his stomach growled. He would take his chances.

Considering the venue, a non-descript steel building erected several decades past, Peter was surprised at the elegance of the luncheon decor. Round tables covered in pale pink cloths were arranged throughout the room, decorated with delicate white vases of pink and white carnations. Place settings of fine china in a pattern of red and yellow roses rimmed with gold dotted the tabletops.

"Hello, Sheriff. You're just in time for lunch," said a middle-aged woman, golden blonde hair in an elegant updo. She gave Zack a dubious look.

"Eleanor?" asked Peter.

"Why, yes."

"Peter. Peter," called a woman across the room.

Peter turned to find Clementine Cordelia Smith. Clem, long retired from ranching, had a degree in forensics and money to spare. She generously supported the sheriff's office forensic needs and relished any chance of helping in an investigation.

"Hi, Clem."

"Come sit with us. A little sheriff's talk will be a nice change from listening to the same old stories." She lowered her voice. "And the other ladies will be jealous. We don't often have men folk at our meeting, especially one so handsome."

Peter cursed the blush spreading from his neck to his hairline. "Sure, Clem." He removed his hat and hung it on a hook by the door. Sometimes the hat was more trouble than it was worth.

"We have a nice variety today," said Eleanor, holding a tray of tiny crustless sandwiches in front of Peter. "Smoked salmon with cream cheese, cucumber and tomato, and chicken salad."

"Yum." Peter chose a creamy sandwich with spots of pink, hoping for salmon. He suppressed a smile when he saw Eleanor 'accidently' drop a sandwich next to Zack.

"Lemon bars and French macarons for dessert. On the house for you today, Sheriff."

"Thanks. Hey, I need to ask you a few questions later."

Eleanor raised an eyebrow. "This isn't a social call?"

"No, sorry. I'm on an investigation."

"Ooooooh. It's been a long time since we've had a good mystery," offered Clem. "Spill the beans. What are you snooping around about?"

Knowing Fred's death wouldn't stay secret long in the small town, Peter gave into the wave of enthusiasm and said in a stage whisper, "Murder."

Momentary silence fell on the room.

Nancy May, resplendent at the next table in a wide-brimmed tea hat draped with purple and gold organza, announced, "I found the body."

Oohs and aahs filled the room.

"Whose body?" asked Clem.

"Fred."

"Fred who?"

"You know. Fred Filmore of the perpetual garage sale."

A serving tray clattered to the floor. "Murdered?" exclaimed Eleanor, broken sandwiches covering her feet. "How awful. Are you sure he was murdered?"

"Autopsy confirmed it," said Peter.

She stooped to clean up the sandwiches, changed her mind, and sat on the chair next to Peter.

"Were you friends?" asked Peter.

"With Fred? No, he was a nuisance. Look what he did to that lot next to my shop. I'm fortunate to have such loyal customers. My tourist trade has dropped significantly since he started that mess."

Peter turned in his chair. "Any of you ladies remember seeing Fred past noon on Tuesday?"

"I saw him stringin' those Christmas lights after noon," said an elderly woman in an elaborate tea hat. "That was before he had the balloons flyin' "

"Anyone after that?"

"I was in the shop until four," said Eleanor. "The decorations were up, but he was gone by then. At least he wasn't sitting in that old chair on the boardwalk."

"Did you go out after that?"

"Let's see. I closed shop and went upstairs to my apartment." She thought for a moment. "I made myself an egg salad and cucumber sandwich and went to bridge club at six." She glanced at Peter and explained, "We usually have a light dinner at bridge club, but it was at Margaret's house this week."

"Margaret Franks who owns the quilt shop?"

Eleanor rolled her eyes. "Yes, that Margaret. She's always afraid someone will get something sticky on the cards, so we all get a to-go bag at the end of the evening. I eat before I go."

"When does bridge club get over?"

"Eight o'clock sharp when it's at Margaret's house. Otherwise, we hang around and visit."

"Where did you go after you left?"

"I came home, got into my pajamas, and watched a movie."

"Did you hear or see anything unusual in the lot next door when you got home or during the night?"

She pondered the question. "No, I didn't, but, well, I tend to turn the television up too loud, and wear ear plugs when I go to bed. The street noise from the brewery keeps me up otherwise."

"Can anyone confirm you were home after bridge club and until Wednesday morning?"

"Am I a suspect?" said Eleanor, worry creasing her forehead.

"Everyone is a suspect until the murder is solved. I need to ask."

"I live alone. I didn't talk to anyone after I got home."

"Okay, thanks, Eleanor. Call over to the office if any of you think of anything else," he said to the room. Peter finished his salmon sandwich and reached for a cucumber tomato.

"Do you need me for forensics?" asked Clem.

"Not yet. I'll let you know."

Not one to pass on good food, Peter finished his sandwiches and dessert before he donned his hat and said his goodbyes. He whistled to Zack and walked the block back to Main Street, scanning the neighborhood for the next possible witness.

Across the street, he saw Holly instructing a table of kids how to sift buckets of dirt for sapphires. Peter groaned inwardly. Talking to Holly had become awkward since he acknowledged to himself that he would never have a future with her. More frustrating was the fact that she had no idea anything had changed. Holly had moved on several years ago when, in a fit of rage, she threw his offered engagement ring in his face. Unless, of course, she needed his help with something. In Holly's mind, he should always be there for her, regardless. He kept telling himself the next time the answer would be "no."

"Hey, Holly," he said as he arrived at her table.

"Oh, hi, Peter." She nodded and then went back to the lecture.

"Are you about finished? I need to ask you a few questions."

She looked at him, surprised. "Uh, sure. Just a few more minutes." She finished her talk and motioned for her assistant, Matthew, to take over kid duty.

"What's up?"

"Investigating Fred's death."

"Fred died?"

"Did the town gossip mill shut down? Normally this stuff is all over the county before I know what's going on."

"Fred is... was an annoyance. Most of us avoided him. Good riddance, really. How did he die?"

"Murder."

"Murder? Who would murder Fred?"

"So far, everyone I talked to couldn't stand the guy, and yet, everyone is surprised he would be murdered. Explain that."

"Well... it's true he was a despicable creature, but murder? It takes a lot of rage to commit murder. Unless the murderer was a psychopath. Is there a psychopath running loose in town?"

"Please don't spread that theory around. It will have the mayor and Mavis inciting terror throughout the county."

Anderson's less than competent Mayor Kalinski, and Mavis Vallee, owner and editor of the local paper, *The Anderson Chronicles,* spent more time chasing after publicity than serving the public.

"I'm surprised they haven't already called a press conference," said Peter. He had dubbed the pair, *M&Ms* for a short time and then realized neither one was sweet or desirable.

"How? When? Why?" asked Holly. "Come on. Give me the dirt."

"How? I'll keep how to myself for a while. It's part of the investigation. When is some time between Tuesday afternoon and evening. Why? Good question. Like I said, he was unanimously disliked."

"So, what do you need from me?"

"When was the last time you saw Fred?"

She thought. "I didn't see him string those lights or float the balloons. I was at the dig site with a group. I didn't see him when I got back... remember, you and Angus came by looking for him?"

"I remember."

"I guess the last time I saw him was Tuesday morning. He was sitting in that old chair in the middle of the boardwalk."

"Do you remember anything unusual that day?"

"Other than the Christmas lights and balloons? No."

"Was Matthew here helping on Tuesday?"

"Sure. He's here full time now. He hired a manager for his gem shop in Missoula and moved here to work for me."

Peter stifled momentary jealousy and reminded himself that he didn't care.

"He wouldn't have seen anything though," said Holly. "He came to work just in time to climb onto the bus. Fred was sitting in his chair at that point."

Peter questioned Matthew and verified Holly's story.

A defunct bakery stood next to The Sapphire Pit. Seeing a '20 Percent Off Sale, Today Only' flag flapping in the breeze, Peter asked Holly, "What's going on over there? I thought Margaret bought the building to use for quilting retreats."

"She did. After the first retreat, she realized decades of butter and brown sugar were embedded in the walls. Too many of her clients complained about grease spots on their material. She sold the building to an antique dealer a few months ago." Holly looked at Peter and laughed. "You need to get out of your office more often."

Ignoring her jibe, he walked down the boardwalk to the new antique store. A bell chimed when he opened the door and a thin, nervous man hurried to the front of the store. He paused briefly when he saw Peter. A flash of loathing crossed his face, promptly replaced with an exaggerated smile. At Peter's side, Zack growled.

"Good afternoon, Sheriff. What treasure can I tempt you with today? Twenty percent off the entire store."

"Peter Elliott," said Peter, holding out his hand. "I'm not shopping."

The same look of loathing flickered in the man's eyes. He reluctantly held out his hand. "Richard Bale."

Contact was brief by mutual agreement. Peter had the urge to wash his hands afterward. "I'm told you've only been in business a few months."

"At this location, yes. I've been in the antique business for several decades."

"Where did you live before this?"

"Am I being interrogated for a particular reason or is this your idea of a warm welcome?"

Peter watched the other man closely. "I'm conducting a murder investigation."

Richard Bale's face showed no emotion. "Oh, my. A murder in Mayberry?"

"No, in Anderson. Are you familiar with Fred Filmore, the proprietor of the rubbish lot across the street?"

"Oh, yes, I'm familiar with Fred, if only to avoid him."

"Did you have much contact with him?"

"None at all, after our initial introduction. He attempted to 'partner up,' as he put it. I told him we were of entirely different social standing and a partnership was impossible. I believe I may have insulted him."

"Did you dislike Fred?"

"I didn't give Fred enough thought to dislike him. I didn't appreciate the eyesore, but it kept legitimate business on my side of the street. I should have thanked him."

"When was the last time you saw him?"

Richard thought for a moment. "Tuesday, I think. Yes, Tuesday at lunch time. I left the shop and walked over to the brewery food truck for a burger. I remember seeing him because he was hanging those ridiculous lights and balloons."

"You didn't see him after that?"

"Not that I recall. I left at five, but I park in back so didn't notice what was going on across the street."

"Did you see anyone suspicious hanging around?"

"No more than the usual tourist traffic."

"Okay. Where were you from Tuesday at five until Wednesday morning?"

"You can't think I had anything to do with that slob's death. Why would I bother?"

"Just answer the question."

"Well, as I said, I was here at the store until five on Tuesday and then home. I was home all night."

"Do you have any witnesses?"

"No. I live alone."

"And where is home?"

Richard huffed and rolled his eyes. "I'll write out the address." He took a business card off the counter, flipped it over, scribbled an address, then handed it to Peter.

Peter folded the card and slipped it into his shirt pocket. "We'll be in touch."

Richard Bale watched with an odd mixture of curiosity and apprehension as the Stone County sheriff and his dog walked out the door.

⁂

BACK IN HIS cozy office, Peter gathered the crew for an update. "Doc is estimating the time of death between one thirty Tuesday afternoon to nine thirty that night. He also believes it was raining when the body was dumped at the landfill and covered with grass. The rain started around one o'clock Wednesday morning, so if Doc is right, the body was dumped after that. Between death and being dumped, the body was lying naked in a prone position." He glanced at the crew. "On his stomach. Lividity and blanching was in a diamond pattern."

Angus cleared his throat, worried that he was the only one who didn't know what lividity and blanching meant.

Peter explained and then said, "Fred's body was lying face down, naked, on something hard with a diamond pattern for at least twelve hours before it was dumped."

"What could cause a diamond pattern?" asked Helen.

"How about a patio table," said Travis. "Some of those metal ones have a diamond cut-out pattern."

"Good thought," said Peter. "I'm not sure Fred would fit on a patio table, though."

"It would go along with the grass clippings and plastic pool."

"True. Could you look into that tomorrow, Angus? Find out if anyone is missing a kiddie pool and has a recently mowed lawn."

"Sure, Boss."

"How'd the interviews go?" asked Helen.

"I talked to the ladies at Eleanor's Tea Shop and the new antique store owner, Richard Bale. Eleanor and Richard both live alone and have no one to verify that they were home Tuesday night. Phil Meyer, on the other hand, is married. Could you verify with his wife, Pam, that he was home after work and all night Tuesday?"

"Sure."

"Other than that, the general consensus is that nobody liked Fred, but nobody had a good enough reason to murder him."

"So they say. Someone wanted him dead," observed Angus.

"It doesn't feel premeditated though. This was an act of rage... to stick a fork in someone's brain..."

8

THE SHRILL BLARE of a fire alarm woke Peter from a deep sleep. He rubbed his eyes, groaned, and looked at his bedside clock. Three fifteen. *Why can't this stuff happen in the middle of the day?* On cue, his phone pinged. Birdie.

Birdie Bradshaw, as the newest Stone County deputy, worked night shift. He read her text message. *Fire at the landfill. Sounds like that Fred guy's house. I'm heading out there.*

Any other fire, he would let Birdie and the county's volunteer fire department handle things. This was connected to a murder investigation. He gathered yesterday's uniform off the straight-backed chair by his bed and dressed in the kitchen while a cup of Earl

Grey boiled in the microwave. He poured the tea into a to-go cup and whistled to Zack.

The taste and smell of ash assaulted his senses long before he arrived at Fred's place. A plume of smoke led the way. The rutted dirt road was blocked with rescue vehicles and fire trucks, so Peter parked in the landfill parking lot, let Zack out of his kennel, and walked to the burning house.

Rick Jones, Stone County animal control officer, also served as chief of the volunteer fire department. He saw Peter and met him halfway down the hill.

"What can you tell me, Rick?"

"Definitely arson. We found one empty gas can, but it could have been here before the fire. It would have taken more than one. Even with a house this old, the fire wouldn't burn as hot without help."

"Fred was a hoarder. The house was stacked full of paper."

"Even so... it's a complete loss. All we can do is control the fire so it doesn't spread."

"Who called it in?"

"Your new deputy. Birdie."

Peter saw Birdie watching the flames consume the old house and motioned her over. He was amazed how in the wee hours of the morning, after a long shift, she managed to look like a movie star. Her coal black hair and creamy skin glowed in the fire light.

"Good call, Birdie. How did you notice the fire?"

"I was on patrol and smelled smoke. I drove up toward the cemetery and could see flames from there. There's that campground in this direction, but it looked like more than a campfire, so I headed this way to check it out."

"Did you see anything suspicious? Pass any vehicles on your way?"

"Strangely, no. Whoever started the fire hot-tailed it out of here as soon as they lit the match."

Peter watched as flames devoured the old house. *What evidence was being consumed? What did he miss?*

A familiar voice pulled him out of his reverie. Linda and Paul stood at his side holding boxes of food packets and thermoses of hot drinks.

"We brought sandwiches, cookies, coffee, and tea."

"Thanks, guys, but how did you even know we were out here?"

"I heard the fire trucks go by and looked out the window to see which way they were headed," said Linda. "After that it was easy to find with the flames and flashing lights."

"Is this Fred's house?" asked Paul. "The guy who was murdered?"

"Yep."

"Someone burning the evidence?"

"That's what I'm thinking. Fred was into something bigger than garage sales."

Birdie smiled. An associate degree in criminal justice under her belt, but still waiting for a basic training course opening at the police academy, she was eager to prove herself. If she could crack the mystery of Fred's murder, it would solidify her position in the department. "Hey, Peter. Being on night shift, I missed all the dirty details. Can you fill me in?"

Peter chose a sandwich from the box and poured himself a cup of hot tea. Birdie did the same and listened closely to the particulars of Fred's death.

"Have you seen anything suspicious going on at night?" asked Peter.

"No. The usual drunks at closing time. The Roost is always suspicious, but in a back-alley-drug-deals sense."

The local dive bar, Rustler's Roost, began its days as a hideout for cattle rustlers, considered the lowest of the low in the old west. The closest modern-day patrons came to a cow was steaks and hamburgers fresh off the grill, but they actively strived to retain a despicable reputation as a matter of pride.

Thinking of the Roost, Birdie also thought of one person in town who had a bead on Stone County's criminal element. "Hey, thanks for the info. Do you need me here anymore, or can I take off?"

"Go ahead. The fire crew has things under control. Rick will lead the investigation. There's nothing left to do, but watch it burn."

Birdie drove back into town. Rather than going down Main Street, she turned into the alley behind the Roost. On the back side of the lot, behind the bar, sat a simple house of sturdy red brick. The house was old, but well-kept. Mary, the owner of the house and the manager of Rustler's Roost, had no last name that Birdie knew. In a small town, often a first name or nickname was sufficient. *Mary at the Roost* was all anyone needed to know.

Birdie parked in the alley and contemplated her approach.

In most aspects, Birdie and Mary were opposites. Loving and doting parents raised Birdie. Beautiful from the day she was born with raven hair and sparkling green eyes, she spent her younger years pampered and indulged.

Nobody had ever called Mary pretty, not even as a child. As she grew and the soft features of her baby face shaped and hardened into their permanent form, her rating on the attractiveness scale plummeted. A prominent nose, dark beady close-set eyes, and the lack of an obvious chin gave her the profile of a large bird.

Mary never knew her father. Her mother focused her attention on alcohol and whatever was required to feed that addiction. Mary's needs were not a necessity. At fifteen, weary of her mother's drunkenness and endless string of dirt-bag boyfriends, Mary studied a map of the United States hanging in her school library. She traced her finger to a point far from her home in the deep southeast, helped herself to her mother's rainy-day cash stash, and bought a bus ticket to Montana. She landed in Anderson at Rustler's Roost. There she stayed and grew and flourished under the watchful eyes of a band of thugs.

In spite of being the queen of the Roost, which made her by default the queen of Anderson's underworld, Birdie believed Mary to be an honorable person.

A flagstone path bordered by wildflowers led the way from the alley around the house to Mary's front door. Birdie pushed the doorbell. Too late it occurred to her that the queen of the underworld probably wasn't awake until after noon. She turned away, vowing to return at a more polite time.

Mary stood behind the door, fully dressed and alert, studying the deputy with resignation in her heart. She had a decent relationship with the sheriff's office, but decades of living in the underworld made her wary of unannounced visits from law enforcement. She pasted on a fake smile and opened the door. "Birdie, right?"

"Yeah, um... hi. I thought you would still be in bed. Late nights at the Roost and all."

Mary laughed. "I have other people running things these days. I do the books during the day and sleep like a baby at night." She opened the door further. "Would you care for a cup of coffee?"

"That would be great. I'm the low man on the totem pole at the sheriff's office so up all night. Coffee's about all that's keeping me going at the moment."

Birdie stepped into a charming mix of modern and museum.

"Are these original furnishings?" she asked.

"Some. I restored what I could."

"But everything looks so bright and new."

"Some of it is. The curtains and rugs are designed to look period. I like the look but couldn't see keeping the stained and dusty originals. My nostalgia only goes so far."

Mary led Birdie into the kitchen. Like the living room, it had the air of another era with a modern touch.

"Nice," said Birdie, admiring deep farmhouse sinks and a built-in pantry.

Mary opened a cupboard underneath the countertop revealing a hidden dishwasher. "All the modern conveniences hidden behind cupboard doors."

"Did you do this all yourself?"

"As much as I could. I was eighteen and broke when I moved in. Refinishing the furniture required more hard work than skill, although I took advice from anyone willing to spout." Mary handed Birdie a large ceramic mug filled with rich black coffee and gave her a quizzical look. "What brings you here today? I'm guessing this isn't a social call."

Birdie sipped her coffee, swallowed, and cleared her throat, uncertain where to begin. "I was thinking about the serial killer. The one who kidnapped all those girls and left them in the cave to die."

Mary winced. "I still have nightmares."

"Me, too." The bones of Birdie's friend Selina, whose disappearance led Birdie to go into law enforcement, were identified in the killer's cave. Not so for Mary's friend, Faith. "We might not have found Stacey Nichols in time if you hadn't figured out who kidnapped her."

Mary blinked back tears for Faith and nodded. "Thank you. That means a lot."

"The thing is," began Birdie. "Well... I was wondering if you would be interested in helping me with another investigation."

"Me?" said Mary, unable to contain her surprise. "Not another kidnapping, I hope."

"No. Nothing like that."

Mary narrowed her eyes, surprise turned to suspicion. "You know about the code, right?"

"The code?"

"I won't snitch on Roost patrons. They would destroy my business and then me."

"But you snitched on the kidnapper," said Birdie, confused.

"He wasn't one of us. He was on the fringes. Besides, nobody's going to stand up for a serial killer."

"I don't think this case has anything to do with your clientele. I was hoping you might have heard something, though. Something people won't talk to the sheriff's office about."

Mary considered. "Okay, shoot. No promises, but I'll listen."

"You've probably heard about the murder of Fred the garage sale man?"

"Who hasn't. We don't waste a moment of excitement in this town."

"Have you heard anything about why he was murdered?"

"Not a thing. Drug deals and petty larceny are the stuff that goes on in the Roost. Nobody there is interested in a fat old toad and his pile of garbage."

Birdie laughed. "Why did you call him a toad?"

"That's what everyone called him. 'The fat old toad.' "

"Everyone, like everyone at the Roost?"

"No, everyone like everyone in town."

Birdie filed that information in her *significant tidbits* brain compartment. "Do you go anywhere besides Rustler's Roost? Do you hear gossip anywhere else?"

"I gave up garden club and PTA decades ago," said Mary sarcastically. "Most 'decent' folks aren't friendly to the owner of the local dive bar."

Birdie stood to leave, sensing more hostility than goodwill from Mary. "Thanks for the coffee. I know you must be busy."

"No. Wait. I mean, I could help. I just don't know anything about Fred or who killed him." Mary's loneliness overpowered her distrust of authority.

"Well... I was just looking for information. If you think of anything, let me know."

Mary saw Birdie to the door and watched her disappear around the back of the house, overwhelmed with regret and loneliness.

9

DIXIE'S DINER OFFERED generous portions and the cook was skilled, so it was a rare day when seats cooled between customers. Any deviation from the town of Anderson's daily routine tended to bring more regulars in search of gossip. Peter, fortunate to find an empty stool at the counter on the morning after Fred's house burned, was more interested in chatter than the breakfast special. He ordered anyway. The chef's signature Farmer's Omelet was filled with every type of meat, cheese, and vegetable you could find on a typical farm, not necessarily the same recipe every day. Dixie knew to bring a full teapot—Earl Grey—and keep it hot. Peter tasked himself with sifting through gossip and picking out legitimate information.

Accustomed to friendly greetings and low effort chatter, Peter spun his stool around to face his fellow diners.

"Good morning!" he bellowed to no one in particular.

Several people leaned closer into their plates, shoveling food like starving coyotes. The effect would have been more believable minus the expanding waistlines stuffed into too small booths. An old farmer on the stool next to Peter picked up his plate and joined a group of friends at a booth across the room.

Others glanced at Peter briefly, nervously, before turning back to their plates. Confusion passed over the faces of the remaining friendlies as they returned Peter's greeting.

"Mornin', Peter," said Stony Clairmont, retired sailor, and recent settler in Anderson. He set his plate on the counter next to Peter and laid claim to the vacated stool. "Did you pop all the balloons at somebody's birthday party?"

Peter spun his stool back around as Dixie hurried past on her way to take another customer order, avoiding conversation. "Not that I recall, but I seem to be on the town blacklist. Have you heard anything?"

"Nope, but 'ah spend most a' my time on the mountain. Just came ta' town for supplies and thought I'd treat myself to something besides my own cooking."

"Where's Lizbeth?"

"That rascally pup is gettin' too big ta' ride in the grocery cart and isn't allowed in the diner. I left her in my truck. She'll be expectin' a special treat."

"A doggie bag filled with Dixie's special?"

"Yep," Stony tried to get Dixie's attention, but she deliberately ignored his signals. "Looks like I'm on the blacklist, too."

Eventually Dixie walked past Peter and Stony, setting a Styrofoam take-out box in front of each of them. She turned quickly and walked away, but not before clicking a fingernail twice on top of Peter's box.

Peter nodded at Stony. "Time for us to leave." Outside the diner, he said, "Come sit in my vehicle for a minute. I have a feeling there's something interesting in this box."

Stony followed Peter to his Explorer, where Zack was patiently waiting for his own treat. They opened their boxes as soon as they got into the vehicle. Each one was filled with a fresh order of Dixie's breakfast omelet and all the trimmings.

"Do you suppose I can talk Lizbeth into sharing this?" asked Stony.

Peter held a sandwich-sized ziplock bag, sticky with cinnamon roll goo. "I'm deciding if I should lick this off myself or have Zack do it."

"I hope that came with a cinnamon roll."

"Extra-large and gooey."

"Yummy. What's in the bag?"

"Looks like a note written on a napkin."

"Well, get to lickin'. I want to see what's on that note."

Instead of licking, Peter took a pair of nitrile gloves out of the middle console and pulled them on, less worried about contaminating evidence than getting cinnamon roll icing all over his hands. He slid open the bag's plastic zipper and pulled out the napkin. Written in blue ink was:

I can't let anyone see me talking to you. Meet me at the gates to the cemetery tonight at dusk.

"The cemetery at dusk. Creepy," said Stony.

"The cemetery closes at dusk and, you're right, creepy. Not a lot of people interested in hanging out there after the sun goes down."

"Not even kids?"

"In the summer we'll catch a few up there scaring themselves, but in September on a weeknight... they're too busy with school and sports to be messing around at the cemetery. I hope."

"Do you need backup?"

"I'll be fine. Dixie's an old friend. I trust her completely."

Stony nodded and grabbed the door handle.

"Hey, have you met my brother, Paul?" asked Peter.

"Not that I recall."

"He has a place just outside of town. Give me a call when you're done with your errands. We could head out there and let Zack and Lizbeth run around for a while. I know Zack would enjoy the company."

Stony grinned. "Sounds good. Lizbeth wouldn't mind spendin' some time with a creature that speaks her language. She gets pretty frustrated with Ol' Stony sometimes."

10

S EVERAL FACTORS CONTRIBUTED to the hodge-podge of dwellings clustered behind the charming Victorian houses and stately red brick buildings of Main Street.

There was no town planning committee in the early days. A blacksmith's forge sitting close to a two-track wagon trail was the first building on the new outpost of the vast Anderson Ranch. A cabin for the blacksmith followed close behind, necessary for survival through the brutal Montana winters. Eventually a general store was built, with enough distance between to buffer the noise and dust of the forge. When gold and silver miners arrived, they built houses based on convenience. Close proximity to a stream for water, trees for firewood, and access to mine shafts were main concerns. Endless seasons of snowfall, heaving frost, spring thaws, and human excavation formed an array of sloping hills, steep gullies, and exposed banks of gravel in the foothills of the Moonlight Mountains. As the town grew and streets were formed out of necessity, a few abandoned shacks were demolished. Many remained and streets were built around them, resulting in a rabbit warren of dead ends and narrow alleys.

Townsfolk called the area behind Main Street, "The Burrow." It was a popular habitat among the regular patrons of Rustler's Roost. Rumors of an underground network of escape tunnels and drug dens filtered through the gossip mill. Because of its proximity to Fred's garage sale lot, and high percentage of scoundrels, this was the area Angus searched for a home with a freshly mowed lawn and children missing their blue plastic wading pool. An exercise in ironies considering the lack of lawns or children.

Without an organized street map to follow, Angus began on the outskirts of The Burrow and worked his way in, making a point of phoning Travis first to report his location.

"If you don't hear from me by the end of the day, send in a search party."

"Sure," laughed Travis. "Although chances are they'll toss your body into one of those secret tunnels I've heard about."

Although the town was small, Angus was unfamiliar with areas such as The Burrow. Until recently, he worked for his Uncle Jake, sheriff of the nearby town of Rumsey. Tired of Jake using his political ambitions as an excuse to hold Angus back, he signed on full time with Stone County.

Angus drove slowly over rutted dirt roads, studying small, neglected shacks surrounded by crushed beer cans and rusted-out car frames. Shadows flitted behind windows. Watchers. An occasional resident sat on a sagging front porch, glaring at the sheriff's vehicle rolling past. Angus had no doubt if he stopped and questioned these people that he would get the typical Rustler's Roost attitude. *We know nothing. We saw nothing.*

Convinced he was wasting his time and bored silly, Angus smiled in surprise when he turned a final corner onto a street lined with tidy well-kept cottages. In contrast to the rest of The Burrow, this street had an air of charm. Each house was painted a different pastel shade accented with white trim. Guardians sat in rocking chairs on covered porches, sipping cool drinks and indulgently watching over young children playing in yards edged with white picket fences. Older children road bikes or hopscotched on perfect sidewalks outside the fences.

This feels like the Twilight Zone, thought Angus.

He pulled over, parked mid-block, and unfastened his seatbelt while studying the occupants of the closest yard. A young mom smiled and waved from a cotton candy colored front porch. Children flocked to Angus's vehicle, excited at the visit from a sheriff's deputy.

Angus opened his door slowly, careful not to bump an admirer, and swung himself to the ground. "Hi, kids."

"Do you ever turn on your lights and siren?" asked a tow-headed boy Angus guessed to be around five or six.

"Would you like me to?"

A chorus of yeahs and hoots filled the air. Angus laughed and leaned in to switch on lights and siren. Gleeful dancing and whoops rewarded his effort. Not wanting to alienate potential friendly parents, he silenced the noise, but left the lights flashing to entertain the crowd. He locked his doors, turned to the children, and pointed to the friendly woman across the street. "Whose mom is that?"

A sweet dark-haired girl raised her hand and said proudly. "That's my mama."

Angus offered his hand and asked, "Can you take me to meet her?"

The girl grabbed several fingers and led him across the street. She lifted the latch on the gate, but carefully fastened it behind them. "We have to keep the gate locked or Brutus will get out."

"Brutus?"

Angus watched as a large bulldog ambled around the corner of the house, caught sight of Angus, and emitted a low, gruff bark. A spasm of fear shot through Angus, accompanied by memories of a previous vicious dog attack. He was heading to the gate and safety when the dog lay down by the porch steps and began to gnaw on a rawhide bone. A chubby toddler crawled backward down the steps, curled against the large dog, and immediately went to sleep.

"The name Brutus is deceiving," laughed the woman on the porch. "We should have named him Marshmallow."

Angus swallowed his fear and allowed the young girl to lead him up the porch steps. "Howdy, ma'am," he said, holding out the other hand. "Angus McLeod. I'm a deputy with the Stone County Sheriff's Department."

"Carrie Parker," said the woman, giving his hand a quick shake. "What brings you to Haven Way?"

"An investigation. I was driving through The Burrow looking for a missing kiddie pool and a freshly mowed lawn."

Carrie laughed. "Good luck with that. The Burrow's not exactly a bastion of family or lawn."

"I figured that out real quick." He looked around the neighborhood. "Then I found this place. Are you worried about living so close to The Burrow?"

"Not at all. This place started as an offshoot, kids who grew up in The Burrow, but didn't want to live the life. My dad was leader of the thugs back in the day. He bought this lot for my husband and me."

"Does crime seep into the neighborhood?"

"Nope. If anything, they protect us."

Angus considered that belief. "So, you think it would be unlikely that any of your neighbors were missing a blue plastic kiddie pool and a load of grass clippings?"

"As a matter of fact, Mindy Spencer two doors down was looking for a blue kiddie pool a couple days ago. She thought the wind must have blown it into someone else's yard."

"A couple days ago?"

"Yeah. Let's see... today's Friday. I think it was Wednesday when she came by."

The timing's right, thought Angus. "Did she find her pool?"

"Not that I know of."

He gestured left and right. "Which house is hers?"

Carrie pointed to her left. "The yellow house on the other side of this blue one next door. Mindy's probably sitting on her front porch watching the kids. She has a set of twins too young to be outside the fence."

Angus thanked her for her help, gave Brutus a wide berth at the bottom of the steps, and let himself out the gate.

Bored of the light bar, the group of children caught sight of Angus and followed him down the sidewalk. Questions were fired in his direction faster than he could answer. At the gate of the aforementioned sunshine yellow house, Angus stopped and turned.

"Do any of you live here?" he asked.

Many nos and head shakes answered.

"I have some important police business. If you kids stand over on the sidewalk next to my patrol vehicle and wait, I'll have a treat for you."

"Yay!!!!!" yelled the crowd in unison as they ran back down the street.

Angus studied the yard for signs of dog and, not seeing any, let himself through the gate. The yard was empty of toddlers and the porch chairs vacant. He climbed the steps. Stopping in front of the door, he pulled out his phone and typed in a familiar number.

"Hi, Travis. Are you busy?"

"Not so much. What's going on?"

"I have a group of kids here fascinated with the sheriff's department. Could you bring a couple boxes of ice cream bars and some of those Stone County Sheriff Buddy Badges over?"

"Sure. It'll take me a few minutes to stop at the grocery store. I'll be there in a jiffy."

Angus gave him the address. As he slid his phone back in his duty belt, he looked up to find a young woman watching him through the screen door. Her short hair dripped with soap suds and globs of orange muck clung to her T-shirt. A long spaghetti noodle hung from one shoulder.

"Can I help you?" she asked.

"Angus McLeod. I'm from the Stone County Sheriff's Office. Are you Mindy?"

"Yes. Mindy Spencer. Is everything all right?" Worried creases filled her forehead.

"Everything's fine. Your neighbor, Carrie, mentioned that you had lost a kiddie pool recently?"

"Uh. Yeah, but I didn't report it. I just figured it blew away. We had a nasty thunderstorm the night before. The wind was ferocious."

"Did you ever find the pool?"

"No," Mindy laughed. "It's probably in the next county by now. We lose at least one to the wind every year."

"Where did you keep it?"

She opened the screen door and stepped onto the porch. "In the back yard. Why is the sheriff's office so interested in a kiddie pool?"

"There's one connected to a case we're working. I'm trying to track down where it came from."

Mindy glanced toward the door. "The twins are down for their nap. They should be out for a while. I can show you where we kept the pool."

She led him down the steps and around the side of the house. A roomy back yard cluttered with playhouse, sandbox, and assorted toys backed onto a narrow community park. Beyond the park sprawled The Burrow.

A circle of dead grass against the back fence gave away the previous location of the missing pool.

"I try to move it around, so it doesn't kill the grass, but..." Mindy shrugged.

"Do you have security cameras back here?" asked Angus.

"Never felt a need for them."

He nodded toward The Burrow. "You don't worry about those folks bothering you?" He watched her expression go from defensive to sheepish.

"Not at all. Most of us are related to those folks. They protect us better than a security camera."

Angus studied the yard. "It looks like you mowed recently."

"Yeah, well, not me," she nodded across the park. "I pay a guy from over there. I don't have the time and my husband gets frustrated with moving all the kid's stuff out of the way. It's easier to have someone else do it."

"What happens to the clippings?"

"I don't know. He hauls them away. Probably brings them to the landfill. Why?"

"Just curious. I didn't see a recycling bin along the fence."

A shrill cry rang through the air. Mindy gave a tired sigh, "Awake already."

She led Angus around the house to the front gate. "Is there anything else?"

"Could you give me the name of the guy who mows your lawn?"

"Ernie Best. Uncle Ernie to me."

"When did he mow last?"

Mindy thought. "It would have been on Tuesday morning. He moves the pool so he can mow underneath. That's why I didn't notice it gone until Wednesday."

"Do you have his address?"

The crying switched to stereo, and Mindy's walk became a jog. She motioned for Angus to follow her into the house. "Let me take care of these two and I'll write down that address for you."

Angus waited inside the door while Mindy jogged up a stairway to the second floor. He was surprised when she came back without the babies.

"They're asleep again. One loses his pacifier and everyone has to hear about it."

She motioned for Angus to follow her into the kitchen. Two highchairs covered in orange spaghetti debris lined up along the side of a retro metal table. Noodles and sauce covered the floor under the chairs.

"It's times like this I wish we had a dog. It would make cleanup so much easier."

Angus laughed. "You could borrow Brutus."

"I wish. My husband is allergic. If he came home and broke out in a rash the gig would be up."

Mindy pulled a sticky note off a pad on the counter and began drawing. "I'm not sure of the address, but I can draw you a map."

She handed Angus the finished masterpiece. "It's the only house in The Burrow that actually has a lawn. You can't miss it."

Angus let himself out and walked over to his vehicle. Ice cream-covered kids lined the sidewalk, proudly displaying Buddy Badges on their shirts. Travis sat in the middle of the group, holding a toddler on each knee.

"I'm glad I bought extra. Word got out fast and they opened the gates."

ANGUS DROVE TO The Burrow and followed Mindy Spencer's hand-drawn map to the surprisingly tidy yard of Ernie Best. The house sported the typical sagging porch and chipped paint of its neighbors, but the yard was immaculate... freshly mowed, devoid of beer cans or discarded appliances. Under a carport next to the house, a pair of blue jean-clad legs stuck out from under the open hood of a bright orange Husqvarna riding lawnmower. Angus opened his vehicle door and stepped out as a chubby basset hound rounded the mower, crooning a deep mournful tune as he ambled across the lawn. Angus's first instinct, as when faced with all dogs, was to jump into his vehicle and shut the door. On second thought, he realized the slow-moving hound had a slow-moving wag to his tail and was more interested in sniffing dandelions than chasing Angus.

The upper body connected to the blue jean clad legs curled itself from under the hood, revealing an ample belly attached to wide shoulders and a block head. Ernie Best had the look of a once muscular football player gone to seed.

He wiped his hands on an oily blue shop rag as he watched Angus bend to give the dog a two-handed scratch behind the ears. "Careful, Officer, he has a pretty vicious drool."

Angus laughed, "I can see that. He left a trail across the lawn." Angus met Ernie under the carport. "Nice mower."

"It does the job."

"Your niece, Mindy, sent me over. She's missing a blue plastic kiddie pool and thought you may have seen it."

"Things must be slow at the sheriff's office if you're investigating missing kiddie pools."

"The pool isn't the issue. Where it came from and where it ended up is the question."

"She loses at least one of those things every summer to the wind. They usually end up in that park between here and her house, cracked and useless. The city hauls them off with the rest of the rubbish. Most likely they end up in the county landfill."

"Would they haul it to the landfill if it wasn't cracked?"

"I don't know. You'd have to ask the trash collector."

Angus caught sight of a large utility trailer parked behind the mower. "Is that what you use to haul your mower?"

"Yep."

"What do you do with the grass clippings?"

"Am I being investigated for something?"

"Not yet. There were grass clippings involved in the pool issue."

Ernie threw the rag on the ground, kneeled next to the mower, and began loosening the oil plug. He glanced at Angus. "This sure feels like an interrogation."

"Hey, you're the first guy I came across who had access to both a kiddie pool and grass clippings. If you didn't do anything wrong, you don't have anything to worry about."

"There's a gully between here and that community park. I dump grass clippings there. It's a worthless piece of land that nobody uses. Nobody's ever complained."

"Can you tell me where you were Tuesday night?"

Ernie thought. "I worked on lawns all day, then went to the Roost to hang with the guys. I'm sure they'll back me up."

"I'm sure they will," said Angus, knowing perfectly well that the patrons of Rustler's Roost would cover for their buddy. "One more thing. Did you know Fred Filmore?"

"Nope."

"The guy who had the lot full of junk between the Clara Hotel and Eleanor's Tea Parlor? You never heard of him?"

"Oh, the fat toad. What about him?"

"He was murdered on Tuesday night."

"Hmmph. Know nothin' about that." He stuck his head back under the mower lid, ending the conversation.

As Angus walked to his Explorer, he felt eyes following him. Reaching down to pet the dog, he snuck a glance at Ernie. Ernie stared back with an expression of loathing.

11

HELEN PARKED IN front of a two-story cape cod style house on Silver Street, several blocks northwest of Main. Weathered gray shingles, accented with green shutters and white trim blended well with the tidy neighborhood, tidy except for that particular yard. Weeds choked out the remnants of domesticated plants in front flower boxes. Clumps of crabgrass dominated an overgrown lawn, interspersed with bare dirt. Helen knew of Phil Meyer as the manager of the elegant Clara Hotel. She had never met or heard tales of his wife, Pam, but couldn't help wondering what domestic circumstances had led to the neglect of what she assumed was once a lovely home.

Stone steps led to a narrow porch and a wooden door adorned with a brass knocker. Masking tape covered the doorbell, so Helen gave four firm raps with the knocker. As she awaited a response, she listened for signs of life. The other side of the door stayed silent, but if she listened closely, she could hear an occasional strain of music from somewhere behind the house. She left the porch and followed the music around the side and to the back yard where it picked up a decidedly country twang.

A woman sat with her back to Helen on a brick paver patio. Her folding chair edged close to an easel which the woman leaned into, paintbrush in hand, almost touching the canvas with her nose. Helen hesitated, not wanting to startle her. After a few minutes, the woman leaned back in her chair and studied the picture, a cowboy scene in shades of brown.

Helen cleared her throat. The woman jerked in surprise and the paint brush flew into the air. She turned, saw Helen, and grabbed her chest.

"You about gave me a heart attack!"

"I'm sorry," said Helen. "You were concentrating so hard; I wasn't sure how to let you know I was standing here."

The woman took in Helen's uniform and her expression turned from surprise to concern. "Is there something wrong, Officer?"

"No, I'm working on an investigation. Are you Pam Meyer?"

"Yes."

"Phil Meyer's wife?"

"Yes. What is this about?"

"Are you familiar with the murder that occurred recently in Anderson?"

"The guy with the lot full of junk next to the hotel? Yeah. Phil's been ranting about that mess for months. He was thrilled when the guy got whacked." Pam put her hand to her mouth. "That didn't sound right. I mean, he was happy the mess was going to be cleared away."

"Do you mind if I sit down?" asked Helen.

"Sure." Pam waved to a circle of wicker chairs. She stood, retrieved her paint brush from the grass, and dunked it into a brush cleaner on a stand next to her chair. "Would you like a cold drink?"

"That would be great, thanks."

Pam eyed Helen wistfully. "I'm guessing white wine is out of the question?"

Helen laughed. "Not while I'm on duty."

"Darn. I haven't had wine and girl talk for ages. I have iced tea."

"That'll work. Thanks."

While Pam went into the house for tea, Helen stood and studied the picture on the easel. Three cowboys sat around a campfire drinking coffee, unaware of a raccoon stealing food out of a saddlebag.

"The tourists eat those up," said Pam, walking up behind Helen and handing her a tall, frosted glass.

"They're very good."

"Several shops in town carry them. The extra money helps."

Helen sat in her chair and took a sip of tea. Pam's glass held a clear liquid with a slight pink tinge and Helen suspected she had opted for white wine.

"I don't understand," said Pam, bringing the conversation back to murder. "Do you think Phil had something to do with that man's death?"

"Fred Filmore, the victim, was not a popular man. Phil's not the only one in town who was thrilled to see him gone. We have to follow up with everyone who had a grudge against him."

"Phil was annoyed at the mess, but not enough to murder the man."

"Did he have any plans to deal with the situation? Did he ever threaten to harm Fred?"

"Oh, you know, the usual 'I could kill that guy,' but who doesn't say that when they're mad. You can't take that stuff seriously." She took a long sip of her drink and giggled. "Phil comes home every night and sits in front of the television until he falls asleep. Not exactly Mr. Rage and Passion."

"Was he home Tuesday night?"

"EVERY night. Same thing. Dinner. TV. Snoring."

Helen mustered her best wine-and-girl-talk face, gave Pam what she hoped was a knowing wink, and asked, "Does he go upstairs and give you a good cuddle every night, too?"

Pam hesitated a tad too long. "Uh, yeah, you know, after he wakes up."

12

"Howdy, travis," said Dr. Hamm as he strolled into the sheriff's office.

"Hey, Doc."

Dr. Hamm dropped an evidence box on Travis's desk. "Here's the fork, gore and all. I was careful removing it from the victim so as not to smear fingerprints."

"Thanks, Doc... I think," said Travis as he lifted the lid on the box and glanced at the fork. Blood and other matter he preferred not to think about covered its tines. He stifled a gag. "I'll let Helen handle that fingerprint job."

After Dr. Hamm left, Travis sat at his desk staring at the evidence box, a plan forming in his mind. He wasn't an official deputy so he couldn't conduct official investigations, but that didn't mean he couldn't do a little unofficial snooping.

He opened his bottom desk drawer and took out his digital camera. A quick cellphone photo might be easier, but he knew from his forensics training that those pictures were often lower quality, easy to manipulate, and hard to authenticate.

Opening the box and looking through the camera lens long enough to take a decent picture was the hard part. An intolerance for violence and gore is what kept Travis from fulfilling his dream of being a Stone County sheriff's deputy. Feeling foolish, he opened his top drawer, shook a cube of peppermint gum out of a container, and popped it into his mouth. Chewing and peppermint should stifle the gag. He would deal with the image of gore burned into his brain later. He pushed the *on* button on the camera and checked the time and date stamp to verify it was current. Lifting the evidence box lid with his left hand, he held the pointer finger of his right on the shutter button. After allowing autofocus to do its work, he pushed the button. *No gags so far. I can do this!*

Travis took several pictures, connected his camera to the computer, and printed off the best shots. He changed into the street clothes he kept at the office for emergencies, forwarded the office phone to his personal cell number, and folded the photos into his back pocket. The antique store was a quick trip down the hill. He wouldn't be gone long.

⟡

FOOT TRAFFIC WAS heavy that afternoon with many out-of-towners in the market for authentic western antiques. Travis scanned the room but didn't see anyone fitting Peter's description of Richard Bale. He sighed with relief. Thinking about going undercover and actually pulling it off in front of a suspect were two different things. He wandered around until he found the antique silverware display case against a far wall, scanned the room again for Richard, and pulled out the photos of the murder fork. He was having no luck finding a set to match the pattern, but on the bottom shelf he found a similar three-tined fork.

He said, "Aha," more loudly than he meant and jumped when a voice asked, "Can I help you?"

Startled, Travis banged his head against the display case.

"Ouch!"

Rubbing his head, Travis turned to find a thin, balding man glaring down at him, left eye twitching nervously. Richard Bale.

"Were you looking for something in particular?"

"Uh... " Travis glanced at the pictures in his hand and quickly folded and stuffed them into his back pocket. He pointed at the similar fork in the case. "I was curious about that big fork."

Richard sneered, the expression he saved for obvious antique ignorance. "That is a bread fork, circa 1905. Sanderson-Sheffield. The fork is embossed Tudor Rose. The handle, Kings pattern."

"Cool." Travis thought fast. "My... a... mom collects those. I was looking for a present for... ah...her birthday."

"Your mother collects antique bread forks?" asked Richard.

"Yeah... um, yes, she does. How much is that one?"

"Sixty-five dollars. Should I wrap it?"

Travis gulped and tried to recall how much cash he had in his wallet. *Sixty-five dollars for an old fork. Maybe I can sell it to Angus's mom.*

"Yeah. That would be great. Wrap it, please."

⁂

THE CREW GATHERED in Peter's office to share murder investigation notes.

"Well... anyone come up with a clue?" asked Peter. "Yes, Travis?"

"Doc came by and dropped off the fork that killed Fred. Helen dusted it for fingerprints, but it was wiped clean."

"Okay. About what we expected. Helen, did you have any luck with Pam Meyer?"

"Only hunches. She said Phil comes home every night, eats dinner, and falls asleep in front of the television. I suspect she was drinking when I was there and have an inkling she drinks too much on a regular basis... the house had an air of neglect."

"Would she know if Phil left the house on Tuesday night?" asked Peter.

"I doubt it. She hesitated when I asked her about him coming to bed. If he falls asleep in front of the television every night, she's most likely asleep or passed out when he does go to bed. If he goes to bed."

"So, he has a grudge against Fred and a weak alibi. Keep him on the suspect list. Did you find anything, Angus?"

Angus told them about his afternoon in The Burrow and chat with Mindy. "I checked out Ernie Best, the guy who mows her lawn. He mowed on Tuesday morning so had access to her pool and grass clippings."

"How was his attitude?"

"He was friendly enough at first but got snippy when I started asking him about grass clippings. He landfills his clippings in a gully behind his house so may be worried about us coming down on him for that."

"What would be his motive for killing Fred?"

"None that I can think of. Fred's mess in town wouldn't bother him. He lives in The Burrow and mows lawns."

"Does he have an alibi for Tuesday night?"

"He said he was at Rustler's Roost, and they would vouch for him."

Peter rolled his eyes. "In other words, he doesn't have an alibi."

"Nope."

"And questioning his neighbors will get us nowhere."

"Nope. They're all from the Roost gang."

Peter sighed. Another murder case with dead-end clues.

"Oh, yeah," said Angus. "On my way out of The Burrow, I drove through the alley behind Fred's lot. There's a beat-up blue cargo van parked back there. I ran the plates. It's registered to Fred."

"Well, that's something," said Peter. "Any sign that it had been driven recently?"

"There weren't any tracks in the mud, so he didn't drive it after the rain, but there was a half-full bottle of pop in the console and food containers from the food truck. I'd guess it's the vehicle he drove regularly."

"Rather than the Chevy truck we saw at his house. That points toward him being murdered in town. Helen, process the van. See if it can give us any clues."

"Will do."

"I'm meeting Dixie at the cemetery at dusk," added Peter.

"Dixie at the cemetery at dusk," Helen repeated with raised eyebrows. "Isn't that where all the high school sweethearts go?"

"It's not like that." Peter explained about his breakfast at the diner and the snubbing by certain patrons.

"Weird," said Helen. "Do you think it has something to do with Fred's murder?"

"I don't know what else to think. That's the only thing unusual going on in town."

"Hey, Travis, see if you can find out anything about that guy running the new antique store. Richard Bale. There was something off about him."

Travis laid the antique fork, still wrapped in its box, on Peter's desk.

"What's this?"

"I went to the antique store today. Just to see if they had anything that matched the murder fork."

"You did what?!"

Travis gulped. "I changed my clothes so he wouldn't know I had anything to do with the department. I didn't ask him any questions." He hung his head. "I was just curious, that's all."

Peter opened the box and studied the fork.

Travis said, "It's not a design match, but that's the same type of fork. He said—"

"That it was an antique serving fork," offered Angus. "I knew it."

"An antique bread fork, specifically. Do you think your mom would want to buy it from me?"

Angus laughed. "Set you back more than you expected?"

"Sixty-five bucks! For an old fork. Go figure."

Angus pulled out his wallet, separated three twenties and a five, and handed them to Travis. "I'll give it to her for Christmas. She'll be thrilled."

"Thanks, Angus."

"Back to Richard Bale," prompted Peter.

"He's either led a very sheltered life, or that's not his real name," said Travis.

"Why do you say that?" asked Helen.

"There's not only no record of legal troubles, there's no record period. No driver's license, no real estate transactions. Margaret didn't sell him the building. She rents it to him. I called her. He pays in cash. On time. Every month."

"Interesting," said Peter. "I don't suppose Margaret checked his ID before signing the contract?"

"Nope. She was thrilled to have a reliable renter. And he did sign as Richard Bale."

"I have a hunch if we ran his prints, they would come up hot." Peter studied the antique fork, still nestled in its box. "Hey, did he wrap this for you?"

"Yes, he did. And no one else has touched it since I bought it," said Travis with a grin. "I'll check for prints and run them through IAFIS."

"Perfect! Maybe we'll actually have a case with a clue."

"Should we ask ourselves who had access to an antique serving fork?" asked Helen.

"Just about anyone," said Angus. "Richard Bale and anyone who's been in his store. All the ranchers in the area living in old farmhouses with silverware drawers. Anyone with grandparents who still use their wedding silver."

"True. We'd be chasing our tails on that one."

"Anything else going on I should know about?" asked Peter.

"Not even a call about cows on the road," said Travis. "Uh... did you see this week's paper?"

Peter sighed. "No. What's Mavis up to?"

"A front-page spread calling Anderson 'The Montana Murder Capital.' "

"At least she didn't call the television station."

"Not yet. They'll pick it up soon enough."

"Ignore it for now," said Peter. "Local folks don't take her seriously. We'll deal with outsiders when they show up."

Peter's phone pinged. "Hey, Stony. All done with your errands?"

"And then some."

"Meet me in the courthouse parking lot."

"Already there."

Peter whistled to Zack and headed for the door. "I'll be out for a bit, but available if anyone needs me."

Travis gave him a thumbs up. "Sure, Boss."

LIZBETH'S SHORTER LEGS struggled to keep up and, occasionally, she would stumble and roll. Zack waited patiently while she pulled herself upright.

"They'll sleep well tonight," commented Paul.

Peter, Stony, Paul, and Linda sat on the deck drinking apple cider and eating pumpkin cookies.

"From your pumpkin patch?" asked Peter.

"From a can. I tried processing the pumpkins once and decided it wasn't worth the bother. We sell them at the church fall festival instead," said Linda. "Someone else does the work and the proceeds go toward the Christmas food baskets. Win. Win."

"Canned or otherwise, it's the best cookie I've 'et in a while," said Stony, grabbing his third from the tray.

"Don't fill up on cookies," warned Linda. "I have a big pot of white chicken chili bubbling on the stove. You two are welcome to stay for dinner."

Peter cleared his throat. "Actually, I have to go. I have sheriff stuff to do."

"Aren't you off duty soon?" asked Linda

"You know how it is. We're never really off duty."

"Well, I hope you'll stay," said Linda, turning to Stony.

"Wouldn't say no to home cooking that's not my own."

After Peter and Zack left, Lizbeth curled up at Stony's feet and went to sleep.

"This murder is getting to him," said Stony, watching Peter drive away.

"Murders always do. He starts brooding about our parents," said Paul.

"Your parents?"

"They were murdered when we were just kids."

"Gosh, that's a heck of a thing."

"It happened in Missoula. They were celebrating their anniversary." Paul took a sip of cider to collect himself. "Mugged in a park."

Linda took over for Paul. "They were shot."

"For a few dollars. That's what their lives were worth."

"The boys came to Anderson to live with their grandparents."

"Gramps and Nanna weren't in the best of shape themselves, not for raising two rambunctious boys anyway. The local sheriff helped out... kind of a surrogate dad. He took us camping... fishing... that sort of thing."

"It's been Peter's goal to find the murderer... really, that's what led him into law enforcement."

The three sat and sipped and pondered, appetites lost to sorrow.

13

SUMMER SLOWLY EASED into autumn. Shorter days, leaves changing from green to gold, and the whistles and grunts of practice coming from the high school football field. Like the rest of the sheriff's crew, Peter kept a change of civilian clothes available in the office. After everyone else left, he pulled on hiking boots, shorts, a T-shirt, and his favorite fishing hat.

As Peter whistled for Zack, his desk phone rang. He contemplated ignoring it, but the possibility of a true emergency won the debate.

"Peter Elliott. Sheriff's office."

"Hey, Peter. This is Holly. There's something crawling around in my attic and it's a lot bigger than a mouse."

"And... "

"And I need you to come and take care of it."

"Sorry, not tonight."

"What do you mean?"

"I'm not available to help you with that. Did you try animal control?"

"It's after five. You're off duty."

"Which is the first reason I'm not available. The second is I have other plans, and the third is removing critters from attics isn't in my job description. Call animal control."

"Why are you being so awful?"

"I'm being reasonable, Holly. If you don't want to call Rick at animal control, call Angus. I'm sure he would be glad to help."

Dead air echoed in Peter's ear when Holly disconnected without another word. A bittersweet smile crossed his face as he set down the receiver. He had finally let go.

Peter used the rear stairway to leave the courthouse. He would rather have hiked to his cabin in the Moonlight Mountains for the night, but a murder investigation took top priority. He had a meeting with Dixie at the cemetery.

Too many noses in other people's business was a blessing and a curse when living in a small town. Some folks knew your troubles and were there to help, others knew your troubles and gleefully spread embellished gossip for their own amusement or need for attention. Peter didn't want to take the chance of anyone noticing he and Dixie were both heading for the cemetery at the same time. The hike was a cover. He packed a cold dinner for Zack and himself, along with a paperback to keep himself entertained while he waited for Dixie. Fortunately, the same trail that led from the edge of town to his cabin eventually veered off toward the cemetery. Prying eyes would see him heading up the mountain and lose interest.

Zack chased rabbits and squirrels, and splashed through the creek that followed the path. Peter walked, head down, brooding over the recent murder and arson. Fred was not well liked, but not what Peter would consider murder material. There had to be a deeper issue at play. The burning of Fred's house reinforced that theory. Fred was dead, so burning his house wouldn't hurt him. What was the arsonist trying to hide?

Inside the cemetery gates, several benches formed a semi-circle facing the statue of a trail weary cowboy scouting the horizon for stray cattle. This is where Peter sat and watched the road, too engrossed in his thoughts to concentrate on his book.

As the sun began to dip below the horizon, a plume of dust rose along the dirt road leading from town to the cemetery. Before long, a red Mustang Peter recognized as belonging to Dixie topped the ridge.

Dixie pulled into the gates, parked across from the statue, and waved a greeting to Peter as she exited her car with two large drink cups and a bag holding take-out boxes. Peter's stomach growled at the sight of food. So engrossed in contemplating Fred's murder, he'd forgotten to eat his cold sandwich.

"I hope you're hungry," said Dixie. "I brought loaded cheeseburgers and double helpings of onion rings... and an extra burger for Zack."

Zack followed at her heels, drooling.

"My favorite!" said Peter. "And apparently Zack's too, although you could bring just about anything, and he would be drooling."

Dixie sat next to Peter and handed him a box. "It's been a long time since we hung out up here. I miss those days."

"Me too. Who would have thought our best memories would be of the cemetery."

Dixie giggled. "I've been thinking about it all day. Remember that time we got those bones from the butcher and then covered that grave in a layer of dirt, so it looked like it'd been dug up."

"And stuck the bones all over." Peter laughed at the memory as he opened the box, tore off a chunk of burger, and threw it to Zack.

"In a town this size, we probably should have known there was a burial planned for the next day."

"I did feel a twinge of guilt when old lady Custer fainted."

"Yeah, right before you almost fell out of the tree trying not to laugh."

"It wouldn't have been so bad if that dog hadn't run off with a leg bone." Peter snorted at the memory.

"Good thing we didn't get caught. You probably wouldn't have been elected sheriff. Townsfolk don't forget."

Peter glanced over at Dixie, noticing for the first time warm caramel hair falling in a gentle wave across a pixie face. Cornflower blue eyes caught his gaze and smiled. When did his childhood pal turn into a woman?

"Yeah, good thing." He concentrated on chewing an onion ring. "Speaking of sheriff stuff. What did you need to tell me?"

She took a bite of burger, chewed, and washed it down with a drink of pop. "People are so used to me running back and forth around the diner, they don't pay much attention."

"Sure."

"I pick up snippets of conversation. Most of it's what you would expect; kids talking about the football game and the Friday night dance, women talking about their kids and husbands, ranchers talking about cows and crops."

"Anyone bragging about killing the Toad and burning down his house?"

Dixie laughed. "Not exactly, but there's something different going on... those ranchers who huddle together and go quiet when a deputy comes into the diner, like they did to you this morning. I think they're up to something and it has to do with money."

"Okay. Tell me what you're thinking."

"What I know for sure is cattle prices are way down and hay was short this year. Most ranchers can't afford to sell their cows and can't afford to feed them. The ones who live frugally and have their places paid off, tighten their belts and get through the rough years. The ones who aren't so careful with their money are nervous. Bills are coming due."

"And those are the ones who are acting funny?"

"Yep."

"You're guessing they're doing something illegal to raise extra cash?"

"That's what I think. I've heard them talking about antiques and Fred's name came up a few times."

Peter thought about Fred's hoarder house full of garbage and his overflowing junk lot. "I know one man's treasure is another man's junk and all that, but connecting Fred and valuable antiques doesn't fit."

"I've been thinking a lot about that too. Those ranchers live on places that have been in the family for generations. Maybe grandma is still alive and maybe she has a house or barn full of antiques, and maybe she isn't with it enough to know if a few pieces of furniture or precious jewels disappear."

"You think any of that stuff is worth enough to kill someone over?"

"Oh, yeah. Haven't you ever watched those antique shows on TV?"

"No."

"People come in with an old oil painting they found stuffed in a frame behind grandma's prized 'paint and sip' and it turns out to be a long-lost Rembrandt."

"No kidding?"

"All the time. So, these ranchers, maybe their wives, have been watching antique shows and decided the answer to their money problems is to raid grandma's house when she's in town playing bingo. They even offer to drive her, so she doesn't come home and surprise them in the act."

"Makes sense, but Fred as a connection? I went through his house before it burned down. If he was dealing in antiques, he didn't keep them there... or on his perpetual garage sale lot."

"There's that new antique store across the street. What's that guy's name?"

"Richard. Richard Bale."

"Fred. Richard. They both end in d. Could be I misheard."

"That's a stretch. The names are too different. I'm thinking I need to have a chat with those ranchers... and Richard Bale. Now, he strikes me as someone who would be up to no good."

"Anything I can do?"

"Keep listening. And thanks. This is the tip I needed."

"Anytime, Peter. Like I said, I miss evenings at the cemetery."

Peter and Dixie ate in silence, each lost in thought.

"I heard Holly called and asked you to rid her attic of some kind of critter."

Peter glanced at his watch. "Wow a whole two hours and it's already around town. That's impressive even for Anderson."

Dixie laughed. "She came in the Silver Dollar while I was waiting for these burgers, complaining to anyone who would listen." She studied his face. "She said you turned her down."

"There's a first time for everything."

"I was glad to hear it."

"You were?"

"Yeah... Peter?" asked Dixie as she filled her grocery sack with take-out garbage.

"Yeah?"

"We should do this more often."

"Deal." He gave her a quick hug. "On one condition."

"What's that?"

"Can you give us a ride home?"

"Not worried about someone seeing us together?"

He laughed. "I'll duck if anyone drives by. You can drop me off in the alley behind my house."

"Deal."

14

Two a.m. early Saturday morning, Birdie drove down Main Street with the windows open. If she listened closely, she could hear "last call" echoing from one side of the street to the other. She pulled into her favorite watching spot and waited. The larger groups, special occasions, and family get-togethers tended to have designated drivers. It was the singles and couples she watched for. Warm weather usually had a crowd in every bar, but not this night. Summer vacation season was over, kids were back in school, and it was too early for most skiers. Birdie watched a few stranglers, all surprisingly steady on their feet, find their vehicles and follow every traffic law as they made their way down the street. She stifled a yawn.

She had overtime on her timecard with the burning of Fred's house and nothing to keep her on patrol. She toggled her radio button and called into the night dispatcher, Debbie Tonapah.

"Hey, Debbie. There's nothing going on and I'm beat. I'm going home to get some shut-eye."

"Sure, Birdie. I'll let you know if anything happens."

Birdie's apartment was in the opposite direction of where she was aimed. Rather than driving to the end of Main Street and turning around, she took a short cut through the alley. Unfortunately, the alley was blocked by a delivery truck. The truck's cargo door was open, and the lift gate sat idle. There were no workmen in sight, but the door to the building was ajar. Birdie's options were backing all the way out the narrow alley or waiting for the truck to move. She realized the building door opened into the back of Eleanor's Tea Parlor and, remembering the delicious macarons Eleanor served, Birdie decided to check on the delivery men and, at the same time, scrounge some day-olds for an early morning snack.

She found a wide hallway empty of delivery men, but cluttered with antique furniture and cardboard boxes. Not seeing the sort of things she would expect to be delivered to a tea and sandwich shop, Birdie was unable to resist snooping. She wandered through a large room opening to the left. Furniture, boxes, tin signs, and odds and ends of rusted metal pieces covered the floor. More boxes were packed with hastily wrapped glassware. Bubble wrap and cardboard protected paintings lined the far wall. Birdie's cop instincts took over. Something didn't seem right.

⸻ ❖ ⸻

SLEEPLESS IN THE wee hours of the morning, Mary sat on her porch swing, enjoying the quiet of the night. In the mountains, warm fall days cool down quickly at dusk. She zipped her jacket against the chill and kicked the porch floor boards with the toe of her shoe, sending her swing swaying. She thought back to the young deputy who came visiting the morning before. Birdie Bradshaw. Mary's days were filled with booze orders and bookkeeping and the rough men and occasional women who frequented Rustler's Roost. People in her life were employees, customers, or distributors. None were friends. Because of the recent kidnapping case, Birdie and Mary shared a history and understanding that Mary had never had with another human. Birdie came to her asking for help and Mary drove her away. She sat on her lonely porch swing full of regret. But Mary was by nature a problem solver and sitting alone wallowing in self-pity was not a solution. She would find Birdie and make it right.

The patrons of the Roost knew how many deputies the sheriff's office employed, what shifts they worked, and the routes they drove. Like most humans, they were creatures of habit. Because Mary listened, she also knew the routine movements of the deputies and she had a good idea where to find Birdie. Mary's house faced into the alley. Birdie's favorite spot to park and watch for drunk drivers was just a few blocks up the hill. Mary took off walking until she came to Birdie's patrol vehicle parked behind a delivery truck next to the back door of Eleanor's Tea Parlor. Birdie's vehicle was empty, as was the delivery truck. Mary poked her head into the open doorway.

Not seeing anyone, she wandered in calling "Birdie? Birdie? Are you in here?"

Birdie jumped with guilt when she heard a woman's voice calling her name and assumed it was Eleanor. She hadn't meant to be caught snooping. Hurrying toward the doorway, she tripped over a metal oil sign that slid, clanging across the floor. She fell with a thud, pain shooting through her right wrist and knees.

Mary heard Birdie yelp and ran into the room to help. Angry male voices followed. The door to the room slammed shut, leaving Mary and Birdie in total darkness.

"Birdie?" gasped Mary. "Birdie, what's going on?"

"Who is that?"

"Mary. Mary from the Roost."

"What are you doing here?"

"I came to help you with that murder thing."

Birdie pushed herself up with her good wrist. She couldn't see the other one but could feel it and imagined the worst. Locked in a dark room with a broken wrist and a civilian would not look good on her record.

15

R ICHARD BALE SEETHED. Decades of a cautious undetected life of crime were about to come to an end, but he wasn't going down without a fight.

The two punk kids who drove a delivery truck across the Midwest, filling it with stolen antiques and unloading in Anderson, were near hysteria.

"A cop! You shut a cop in that room! I'm not going to prison," yelled the grungy one. Well, they both were grungy.

Richard ignored their ranting. He stared at the patrol vehicle sitting in the alley. *Do those things have tracking devices? It was that new woman deputy. Did anyone know she was here?* He walked over and looked into Birdie's open driver's side window. The keys were hanging in the ignition. *Rookie move.*

"Shut up!" he yelled at the hooligans. "We, and when I say *we*, I mean *you* need to get rid of that vehicle." Richard pointed at the least agitated of the two hooligans. "YOU! Get in this vehicle. YOU!" He said pointing at the other one. "Stow the lift and close the cargo door on that truck."

The men did as they were told, thankful to have someone take charge.

Richard turned to the hooligan driving the truck. "Drive out of town. Stick to the alleys." He turned to the one now seated in the patrol vehicle. "Follow him. When you get a few miles out of town, find a dirt road. It shouldn't be hard. This godforsaken country has more dirt roads than paved ones. Go down a few miles, dump the patrol vehicle, and then come back here."

"No way!" yelled the truck driver. "You're gonna' turn us in. I'm not going to jail!"

"Shut up!" yelled Richard. "I'm not going to turn you in, moron, they'd lock me up too."

He opened his wallet, held it up, and feathered a wad of bills. "I have a job for you, and I need it loaded and out of here tonight. I'll pay twice what Fred was paying."

Both men relaxed at the sight of cash.

Richard pointed toward the building. "Across Main Street is an antique store. Come back into town using the alley behind that store. I'll be waiting for you."

They did as they were told. Richard wasn't worried about them getting caught and squealing. They didn't know who he was. If they didn't come back in a timely manner, he would be long gone before anyone could trace them to him. He was more worried about the sheriff missing his deputy before he got out of town.

Richard watched the truck until it was out of sight. He went back into Eleanor's shop and checked to make sure the padlock was tightly closed on the room holding Mary and Birdie. Then he locked and closed the back door and hurried to his own shop across the street, careful not to let anyone see him. There wasn't time to pack everything. He would have to choose the most valuable.

RICHARD BOUGHT AND sold stolen antiques. It was the only job he'd ever known besides a very short stint flipping burgers as a teenager. It took one shift and a bully of a boss to convince him he wanted more out of life, and that didn't involve hard work or bosses. Walking home that night from the burger joint, he stumbled on a couple guys and a delivery truck and asked what they were doing. Sensing a creature of the same ilk, they took him on and taught him the business.

Decades later, at the top of his game, Richard let greed take control. Oh, he was greedy, he didn't deny that, but he wasn't a gambler. Extreme caution kept him out of trouble, until he heard murmurings of a motherlode of top-notch antiques coming out of a tiny little town in Montana. One more big hit was all he needed. One more hot location and he could spend the rest of his life sipping rum punch in a tropical paradise. There were unknowns, conjectures. Nobody knew who was running the theft ring and nobody knew what to expect from local law enforcement, but general consensus was a small- town sheriff would be more interested in cattle rustling than priceless antiques.

Richard packed up and moved from California to Montana, rented an old bakery building, and kept his eyes and ears open. He would stay in his shop after hours, lights off, and watch. Eventually he saw a delivery truck drive through the alley and stop behind the tea parlor across the street. Watching from the shadows, he witnessed furniture and cartons being unloaded. He found his motherlode.

RICHARD STEPPED INTO the shadows as headlights lit up the alley. The punks were back with the delivery truck.

The men were young and strong from years of loading and unloading heavy furniture and boxes of collectibles. The promise of a bonus for speed kept them on a run.

Richard watched the time. Sunrise came slower in the mountains as the sun struggled to climb the steep peaks. They needed to be out of town and well down the road before light when early risers could witness them leaving. Eventually he said, "Enough." He surveyed his store for anything of value he had missed, ordered his helpers to their truck, and shut the door. He didn't bother to lock it. He wouldn't be back.

Richard pointed the men south and east and assured them he would be following close behind. Trust went only so far. They would get their pay at the end of the road.

16

TOTAL DARKNESS SHOULD have panicked Birdie, but a protective instinct toward Mary overpowered any fear she initially felt.

"Don't worry, Mary. We'll be okay," said Birdie in the most soothing voice she could muster.

"I'm not afraid of the dark," said Mary, with false bravado. "How're you doing?"

"I think I broke my wrist when I tripped." Birdie felt for the transmit button on the police radio clipped to her vest. Dead air. She pushed the emergency button, hoping someone was paying attention. "Can you turn on the flashlight on your cell phone?" she asked Mary.

"Don't have it with me. I left it at home."

"I have a flashlight in my vest, but I can't get it out with this banged up wrist. Can you make it over here?"

"Sure. Sing or something so I can follow your voice."

"Sing?"

"Or hum. Or just keep talking."

Birdie thought of the last song she heard on the radio and started to hum. She heard Mary shuffle her way, sweeping her hands in front of her.

Mary shrieked and Birdie heard her frantically swatting at something.

"Dang! I went through a spider's web. It felt like it was crawling on me." She bumped against Birdie's leg. "I hope that's you."

"It's me. I'm wearing a duty vest. On my right side," she guided Mary's hand, "I have a flashlight in a lower pocket under my arm. Can you feel it?"

Mary awkwardly patted Birdie's body until she felt the hard form of a flashlight. "Got it."

"The pocket is fastened with Velcro. Find the top flap and pull it open."

Birdie heard the rip of Velcro and felt Mary remove the flashlight. "Good. Now feel around the bottom end. The on button is there on the side."

The bright light blinded them momentarily. Mary handed the flashlight to Birdie who switched the beam to low and blinked several times to adjust her eyes.

She stood, walked to the door and worked the latch in both directions. Locked. Coming through in the dark, Birdie hadn't noticed that the door was metal and wider than average. The edges were flush with the wall and tightly sealed. Hinges were on the outside. Giving up on that as a possible exit, Birdie began to walk around the boxes and furniture filling the room, searching for windows or another door.

"Hate to break it to you, but there's no way out of here," said Mary.

"Come on, Mary. Don't give up. Help me find another entrance."

"You don't get it. This building was a butcher shop long before it was Eleanor's Tea Parlor."

"So."

"So, this room was a walk-in meat cooler. I used it as a model for the beer cooler at the Roost. There are no windows. There's no back door. Walls, floor, ceiling, door... they're all made of steel. We're locked in a steel box."

"In other words, we're not getting out of here until someone lets us out."

"Yep. Does anyone know you're here?"

"No. You?"

"Nope."

"I guess that explains why my radio isn't working." Birdie scanned the room looking for comfortable furniture. Her wrist throbbed and she wanted to sit on something other than a cold steel floor. Along one wall she saw an ornate couch upholstered in a gaudy pink pattern from days gone by. Several boxes were stacked along the sofa seat. She pointed and asked, "Do you think you could move those boxes?"

Mary shrugged. She walked over and tested the weight. "Sure." She lifted the boxes one-by-one and stacked them to one side. A cloud of dust billowed around her as she dropped onto one end of the sofa and she sneezed several times. "How long before they notice you gone?"

Birdie sat next to Mary and thought. She realized with a sinking feeling that she hadn't called the stop into dispatch. Debbie thought she was home in bed. "Tomorrow night when I don't show up for my shift... oh... wait. My Explorer is still in the alley. Someone is bound to notice this morning. When does Eleanor open the tea parlor?"

"No idea."

"Still. We just need to get through a few hours until Eleanor gets here."

Birdie's flashlight flickered and died, surrounding them once again in darkness. "Dang. I was so tired when I got off work last night, I forgot to charge my flashlight."

"Who were those men?" asked Mary. "Why did they lock us in?"

"No idea. I was on my way home and saw the delivery truck blocking the alley and the door open. I got nosy and came in here. How about you? Anyone going to come looking?"

Mary sighed. "I doubt it. Not for a while anyway. They'll get worried when payday rolls around."

"When's that?"

"Next week."

Birdie's stomach growled. "Why couldn't we have been locked in Eleanor's kitchen? I've been thinking about her macarons all night."

Mary shivered in the cool of the enclosed room. "I could use some cooking sherry... or even vanilla."

"Really?" Birdie felt a moment of unease.

"Well... yeah. I forgot to have a drink before I came to find you."

"You forgot? How long has it been since you had a drink?"

"Uh... I dunno. A few hours," Mary lied.

Birdie thought back to her own days of heavy drinking. She had never been an everyday, all day long drinker, but some of her party buddies were. Ironically, the fear of DTs kept them drinking.

"Are you afraid of DTs?" she asked.

Mary swallowed hard. "Yeah."

"It takes a while for that to start, though. Doesn't it?"

"I don't know. I never let myself go long enough to find out."

They sat in silence, contemplating possibilities.

"This is how they died, you know," said Mary.

"Who?"

"The girls in the cave. Faith and your friend, Selina. All alone in the dark." Mary felt a tear course down her cheek, imagining the terror of being alone in a cold dark cave with no way out.

An image of dry bones wrapped in rotting clothes and a crystal necklace flashed across Birdie's mind. She shook her head and blocked the image. "This is different, Mary. We're not alone. We have each other. And we're not in a cave in the wilderness. It's just a few hours 'til morning. Someone will find my Explorer and start looking." She didn't mention that she left her vehicle unlocked with the keys in the ignition.

What are the chances it will be there in the morning?

Birdie yawned. "I'm beat. Let's try and get a few hours of sleep." She leaned her head against the high ornate back of the sofa and closed her eyes. Fatigue overcame pain and sent her instantly asleep.

Mary, not so much. Mary's last drink was her lunchtime cocktail. An employee issue had kept her busy at the Roost all afternoon. She decided to forgo her evening nightcap due to an upset stomach. She was sitting on her porch contemplating mixing something to help her sleep when her urge to find Birdie hit and she forgot about the drink.

Restlessness, tremors, anxiety, nausea. Mary knew the beginning symptoms of alcohol withdrawal, and she had them all.

17

PETER STOOD AT the door of the sheriff's office watching his deputies stuff themselves with their morning donuts, and sighed. Comaraderie and routine were good things, but he doubted Helen could chase down a runaway shopping cart, let alone a criminal. As she reached for another donut, he walked over and snapped shut the donut box lid, just missing Helen's fingers, and tossed the box into the trash can. Angus, Travis, and Helen all looked at him openmouthed, too shocked to speak.

"Come on. Let's go to my house. I'll make my famous omelet."

"You have a famous omelet?" asked Angus. "How come I've never heard about it?"

"Well... because I've never made it for anyone before, but it ought to be famous."

"It can't possibly be as good as Dixie's," commented Travis.

"No, and it probably won't ever be famous. In fact, it'll probably look a lot like scrambled eggs and ham. Forward the phones to your cell, Travis. Let's go. We need to have a meeting." He turned and walked out the door, Zack close at his heels.

After exchanging confused glances and shrugs, the crew followed.

Peter's house stood a few blocks from the back door of the courthouse, well within walking distance, but up a hill. Helen was soon panting, and Angus grumbled as mud from the wet dirt road clung to his freshly brushed boots.

At Peter's house, they left their mud-caked shoes on the back porch. The porch opened into a spartan kitchen. A basic 1950s style metal and laminate table surrounded by red and white vinyl chairs filled most of the space. The only wall decoration, a matching red-rimmed aluminum clock.

Helen walked through the kitchen and into the living room while Peter fished in a cupboard for a frying pan. Bare walls and an easy chair with a folding side table dominated the room. A small couch was pushed against a far wall.

Helen called into the kitchen, "Entertain much?"

Peter laughed. "No. I found the chair at a moving sale next door. They threw in the couch out of pity."

He cracked a dozen eggs into a glass bowl, added Alpine spice and cheese, and mixed with a fork. He cut ham slices into bite-sized chunks, threw a few pieces to Zack, and stirred the rest into the egg mixture. The whole mess went into a sizzling frying pan of melted butter.

Angus's stomach growled and Travis wiped a drop of drool from the side of his mouth. Helen searched the cupboard for plates, finding only a couple of mismatched Corelle.

"There's a stack of paper plates in the next cupboard over," said Peter.

"Special for company?"

"Yep."

"How long you been living here?" asked Angus.

"Since I left college. A long time."

"When are you gonna move in?"

Peter shrugged. "I've kind a' been thinkin' about selling ever since I bought the place. Just haven't gotten around to looking for something else."

"Uh... okay. Why did you buy it?"

"Holly and I drove by one day and she said it was cute. I bought it the next day without even looking inside." He gave them a sheepish look. "She dumped me right after that."

Angus perked up and glanced around, ever on the lookout for an in with Holly. "Holly's house is a lot nicer than this."

"No kidding. This place is over a hundred years old. So is the plumbing and electricity. There's no foundation. The floors are laid right on the ground." Peter demonstrated by bouncing on the floor boards. "The only thing that holds it up is the ground is mostly rocks and boulders."

"You could tear it down and start over," suggested Helen.

"I could, but I'd rather find a place with more privacy. The neighbors are so close, they can look right into the windows. Which brings me to why we came here to talk. Privacy."

Helen set paper plates, utensils, and plastic drinking cups around the table and poured orange juice from a carton she found in the refrigerator.

Peter scooped a mound of ham and eggs onto each plate. "Grab a chair and I'll fill you in." He took a few bites, chewed, swallowed, and cleared his throat. "There's something going on in town and I don't know who all is involved."

"Does this have something to do with Fred's murder?" asked Helen.

"That's my guess. Dixie said—"

"So, you meeting Dixie at the cemetery last night really wasn't a date," interrupted Helen.

Peter sighed. "No. She wanted to talk to me but didn't want anyone to see us together. You know how Anderson is, she couldn't risk losing customers because they think she's a narc."

"Too bad. You and Dixie were always a better match than you and Holly."

Peter frowned at her. "Can we get back to business?"

"She nodded.

"Here's the deal. Cattle prices are down, and the hay crop has been skimpy for the last couple years. Local ranchers are struggling financially. Dixie thinks they're selling antiques out from under grandma and grandpa for extra cash."

"What does that have to do with Fred?" asked Angus. "His lot in town is full of junk and his house was a hoarder's paradise."

"I'm not sure. Dixie said some of those ranchers were more upset than they should have been after Fred died."

"Do you think one of them killed him?"

"No idea. Let's review what we do know. Who wants to go first? Helen?"

"We know that Phil Murphy couldn't stand Fred, and his alibi with his wife is shaky."

"He told me his issues had to do with the mess in the lot next door to the Clara Hotel, but claimed he didn't dislike Fred enough to kill him," said Peter. "What can you add, Angus?"

"Mindy Spencer, on Haven Way near the Burrow, admitted to missing a blue plastic kiddie pool and her lawn was mowed recently by her Uncle Ernie Best. As far as I can tell, he had no reason to murder Fred. He claimed not to know him, called him a fat toad when I mentioned the garage sale lot."

"Okay, Travis, did you get any hits on Richard Bale's prints?"

"I sent in a request. Nothing yet."

"Have we heard back from Rick Jones? Does he have any clues about the fire at Fred's?"

"Nothing we don't already know. It was definitely arson. The gas container they found was the same generic red plastic you can buy just about anywhere. No fingerprints."

"Okay. Anyone have anything else to add?"

"Have you thought about Mavis and the mayor?" asked Travis.

"What about them?"

"Well, normally, Mavis would have KRUD TV out of Missoula holding a press conference in front of the courthouse by now. She ran that headline about Anderson being the murder capital of Montana and then dropped the whole thing."

"You think she's involved?" asked Helen.

"I don't know. I just think it's strange she hasn't caused more fuss."

"Bottom line," said Peter, "we can't trust anyone. With the courtroom right across the hallway, there's too much traffic outside the sheriff's office. Don't discuss this case. Unless we're in my office with the door closed."

"Sure," they all said in unison.

"Travis, let me know as soon as something comes through on those Richard Bale fingerprints. He's definitely a person of interest."

"Sure, Boss."

"Can you get me the names and addresses of local ranchers?"

"Uh, yeah. I'll call Mabel at the Chamber of Commerce. Maybe she has a list."

"Good. Get that to me as soon as possible. I'll check off the ones who were acting suspicious at the diner. Angus and Helen can conduct interviews."

"What about Birdie?" asked Travis.

"She won't be doing interviews at night. Will you see her before her shift?"

Travis blushed. "Yeah, she's picking up a pizza from the brewery and bringing it over."

"Good. Fill her in on the case but remind her not to talk about it to anyone, except us."

Travis's phone rang with a forwarded call for the sheriff's office.

"Leave the dishes," said Peter. "Let's get to work."

18

"STONE COUNTY CHAMBER of Commerce. Mabel speaking."

"Hi, Mabel. This is Travis over at the sheriff's office."

"Ugh. What now?"

"Nice to hear your voice, too. How've you been?"

"Still seeing the chiropractor since last time you called. I hope this doesn't involve hauling out old county record books."

"Nope. Just need a current list of local ranchers."

"You think I have stuff like that sitting on my desk waiting for your call?"

"I was hoping you had it in your computer."

"Computer?"

"Never mind. Do you have a list?"

After much grunting, chair rolling, thumping, and slamming of file drawers, Mabel came back on the line. "Okay, I have a list. No guarantee if these people are still alive."

Travis sighed. "It's a start. I'll come right over and pick it up. Thanks, Mabel."

"You owe me one."

The Anderson Chamber of Commerce resided in a squat building across the street from the court house. Travis was out the door and back with the list within minutes. He handed it to Peter, who chewed on a pen while he searched his memory for the faces in Dixie's diner the previous day. He checked off several to be interviewed by Helen and Angus and held one for himself, one he knew he could trust.

"Okay, there's a few to start," he said, handing the list to Helen.

Peter had his own investigating to do. He whistled to Zack and took the back entrance from his office, down the hill to the antique shop. Richard Bale coming to town and opening a shop at the same time as possible stolen antique activity seemed too much of a coincidence.

When Peter got to Richard's shop, all the lights were out.

Odd for the middle of the day.

He scanned the windows and didn't see a 'Closed' sign displayed so tried the door and found it unlocked. The squeak of hinges echoed through a near empty room as the door swung open. Bare display cases and outlines in dust where furniture once sat were evidence of a recently thriving shop. Not everything was gone. Odds and ends of collectibles, mostly glass, sat abandoned on shelves. Well-used toys gathered in corners. Muddy footprints marred once immaculate wood floors.

Peter walked through the store, keeping to the edges of the room, careful not to disturb possible evidence of a crime. There was no sign of Richard Bale in the sales room, storage room, office, or bathroom. Peter found the back door propped open. Deep ruts from the tires of a heavy truck were etched in mud outside the door. He reached for his police radio, but changed his mind. Too many people listened to scanners. He took out his cell phone instead.

"Hey, Boss," said Travis when he answered.

"Travis, can you find contact information for Richard Bale? I'm at his shop, and I can't tell if he's been robbed or he packed up and left in a hurry."

"No kidding. Hold on, I have a copy of his contract with Margaret." Travis opened the Fred Fillmore murder file and leafed through until he found the contract. He began to read off the number.

"Hold on," said Peter. He pulled a small notebook and pen out of his vest. "Okay, shoot."

Travis repeated the number.

"Got it," said Peter. "Thanks."

He disconnected from Travis, punched Richard's number into his phone and waited as it rang. Zack's ears stood up as the ringing became stereo, one from Peter's phone and a tinny twin from somewhere in the building. Richard's phone hadn't been set up to a voicemail, so it kept ringing as Peter followed the generic ringtone through the building. The sound grew louder as he came to Richard's office. Peter found the phone, a basic no-frills model, in a metal garbage can next to the desk.

Burner phone.

He pulled an evidence bag out of his pocket, slipped the phone in, and punched the number for the sheriff's office into his own phone.

"Hey, Boss."

"Travis, could you check and see if Margaret has an extra key for this building? It's looking more and more like Mr. Bale skipped town. I want to lock things up before I leave."

"Sure. I'll check and call you right back."

Peter closed and locked the back door, and waited in the front room until he heard back from Travis.

"Margaret is on her way over with a key. She's not happy."

"Margaret's never happy. Thanks."

Peter disconnected as Margaret burst through the door. She took in the abandoned hodgepodge in the mostly empty room and flew into a rage. "What are you going to do about this, Sheriff?"

"Do about what, Margaret?"

"Do about this mess?"

"Is Mr. Bale current on his rent?"

"W-w-ell, yes. What does that have to do with anything?"

"If he's current on his rent, then no law has been broken. Is there anything in the lease that says he can't remove property or get mud on the floor?"

"... no."

"Do you have an extra key so I can lock the building until we have a better grasp of the situation?"

Margaret reached into her pocket and reluctantly handed Peter a key hooked to a green lanyard.

"When's rent due?" asked Peter.

"The first of the month."

"That's two weeks away. If Mr. Bale doesn't show up by then, you can call it abandoned property. Until then, he's a legal tenant."

Margaret harumphed and stomped out the door.

Peter took one last look around and went through the door, locking it behind him. He stood on the boardwalk and studied the neighborhood. Next door was Holly's sapphire pit. Every table was full of kids and their parents sifting through gravel.

Peter found Holly at a wash trough, dark curly hair barely contained in a ball cap, teaching a youngster how to wash and sift a scoop of gravel for sapphires.

"Hey, Holly."

Holly gave Peter a quick glance, rolled her eyes, and went back to teaching.

"Did you get that critter out of your attic?"

She stopped shaking the screen box and turned toward Peter. "Yes, no thanks to you."

"I had a business meeting, Holly. I can't always drop everything when you call."

She continued to ignore him.

"What did you find up there?"

Holly finished the wash and shake lesson, brought the screen box to the sorting table, and demonstrated how to dump it so the sapphires would be on top of the gravel.

"Holly, I'm conducting a murder investigation and I need to ask you a few questions. We can do it here or at the station."

She whirled around and glared. "Am I a suspect now? Why would I murder that fat old toad?"

"No, Holly, you aren't a suspect. Something is going on at the antique store. I found it unlocked and a good portion of the stock has been removed. Richard Bale isn't there. Did you notice anything unusual?"

"What does this have to do with Fred's murder?"

"I believe there may be a connection. Please, Holly."

Her face softened. "Since you said please. To answer your first question, I called Rick Jones at animal control. Like you, he fussed about coming over after hours, but he at least came. It was a single male raccoon. He tore through a vent... probably looking for a warm nest for winter."

"He cause a lot of damage?"

"Only to the roof around the vent. Angus is going to fix it for me."

Peter smiled. "Good to hear. And the antique store?"

"I've been so busy, I didn't notice it wasn't open. Cold weather is coming fast and families are squeezing in a final bit of summer fun. We even did two runs to the mine today."

"So, have you noticed anything strange at all since he opened?"

"Just that he's not very friendly to locals. People say he has quality stuff, but he's tight-lipped about where he gets it."

"Hey, thanks. Let me know if you hear anything else."

"Sure."

Holly turned back to the sorting lot and Peter went back to the boardwalk. Across the street, he noticed that Eleanor's Tea Parlor was also dark and closed.

He crossed the street. The sign from Thursday was still posted.

Closed Today
Women's Club Luncheon
Community Center
12:00 – 2:00
Eleanor

Weird. Is she sick? The blinds covering the windows were closed. He tried the door and found it locked.

Passing Fred's lot, now roped off with yellow crime scene tape, Peter heard the yip of a dog and a gruff man's voice amongst the clutter. He ducked under the tape and wound his way through cast-off rusty buckets and tables of used clothes until he came upon a rancid man of indiscernible age and his two mangy mutts. Hobo Joe.

"What cha' doin', Joe?"

Hobo Joe jumped and squawked. A piece of scrap metal flew out of his hands.

"You 'bout give me a heart attack, Sheriff."

"This is private property, Joe."

"Yeah, I know. Fred's place, but he's dead ain't 'e?"

"It's still private property. Didn't you see the crime scene tape?"

"Aw, this ain't no crime scene. They done found Fred in the landfill."

"Time to go, Joe."

"Just fer that, I'm of a mind not to tell you what I saw last night."

"What did you see?"

"I was pickin' through stuff. They didn't know I was here."

"Who?"

"That guy what runs the shop across the street and a couple a' hoodlums drivin' a big truck."

"What were they doing?"

"They was unloadin' a bunch a' stuff into the back door over there." He pointed to the back of Eleanor's Tea Parlor.

"Unloading?"

"Yep. Furniture. Boxes a' stuff."

"When was this?"

"Oh, on about midnight. I couldn't sleep so's I was walkin' the dogs."

"Did you see Eleanor?"

"Nope. Jus' thet guy and the hoodlums what drive the truck."

"They didn't take anything out?"

"Nope."

"What did they do after they were done unloading the truck?"

"Don't know. I skedaddled. Thet guy gives me the creeps. I'd be checkin' inta' him fer thet murder ifn' I was you, Sheriff."

"Thanks, Joe." Peter pulled out his wallet and handed Joe a ten-dollar bill. "Here. Go get yourself some lunch."

"Gee, thanks, Sheriff."

"And stay off this lot until we get this murder solved."

Hobo Joe gave Peter an exaggerated salute and hurried toward the brewery food truck.

Peter headed to the back door of Eleanor's shop. He tried the door and found it locked. Zack whined and sniffed around the edge of the door. *Weird.*

Peter filed Zack's reaction onto his mental list of things to ponder, whistled to Zack, and walked back to the courthouse for his Explorer.

19

T WENTY SOME MILES shy of Missoula, Richard clenched his jaw and growled. He followed as the hooligans in the delivery truck slowed and turned onto what Richard considered an unauthorized exit. At the bottom of hill, the truck turned onto a frontage road and pulled to the side. Richard followed in his car, parked, and waited. Tired, cranky, and itching for an argument, he watched as one of the guys walked around the truck and knocked on his passenger side window. Richard pressed a button, lowered the window, and pasted on what he hoped was a disapproving scowl.

"Why did you stop? We didn't discuss a stop."

"Listen, man. We're exhausted. We drove all day yesterday. We've been up all night. There's a rundown motel a few miles from here. We stayed there once on a long run for Fred. They don't get much business so they're not particular about IDs or taking down license plates."

Richard considered. He needed sleep as much as they did, but he didn't want to concede control. He cleared his throat and attempted his best voice of authority. "I can't risk you falling asleep and running off the road. We'll stop, but no messing around. We leave at day break tomorrow."

The hooligan nodded and headed back to the truck. Richard followed as they continued down the road. Eventually they came to an abandoned roadside café, windows boarded up and a faded realtor's sign attached to the door. On the far side of the lot stood a deserted gas station, pumps long ago removed. The sign from the same realtor hung in the window. Logan drove between the buildings to a two-story motor lodge standing at the rear of the lot. If not for the spastic vacancy sign flashing in the office window, Richard would have pegged the motel as abandoned. Overgrown weeds covered the parking lot. Paint peeled away from sagging trim. Several broken and plywood covered windows scattered among twenty rooms, ten along the top and ten below.

Richard parked alongside the delivery truck and followed the guys into an empty office. Richard, tired and impatient, wacked the service bell more times and harder than necessary.

A grubby man in a faded plaid shirt and sweat pants came through a door in the rear, scratching his swollen belly and belching. "Keep 'yer shirt on. Those rooms aren't goin' nowhere."

He glanced at the three men. "How many?"

"One for me," said Richard, pulling out his wallet.

The clerk named a low price. He stuffed Richard's offered cash into his shirt pocket, pulled a stack of clumsily folded sheets and a thin blanket from under the counter, and handed them to Richard. "Ya' make yer' own bed."

Richard stood stunned while the man laid a key on top of the bedding.

"Hey, it's cheap and private," said the man. "If ya' want fancy, go into town."

He pocketed cash from each of the hooligans and handed them their bedding and keys. "Checkout at eleven tomorrow morning. Leave your keys on the counter."

Richard looked at his key fob. Room one. He left the hooligans to their own devices, walked outside to his room door, inserted the key and stiffened in anticipation of a shabby room. He wasn't disappointed. A stained mattress on a metal frame dominated. Richard sniffed the pile of sheets in his arms. At least they smelled clean. He didn't bother to make the bed, instead spread the sheets across the dirty mattress, flopped down and went to sleep.

20

NORTH OF ANDERSON, where hills retreat and the valley opens on both sides of Flint Creek, wide fertile fields grow the variety of grains and grasses needed for plentiful, rich milk production. Milking parlors and equipment sheds of the Geary ranch were tucked in hollows behind the surrounding hills, leaving open areas for farming. As an unintended result, the beauty of the valley from a roadside perspective was retained. A massive stone and log house perched atop a hillside overlooked Geary lands, keeping a watchful eye on the empire.

Peter made his way up the meandering driveway. Typical of most ranch houses, parking consisted of where your vehicle happened to stop. He pulled onto a bare area of the ranch yard, braked, and shut down his motor. Missing was a greeting by a ranch dog or four. The yard was empty.

The doorbell chimed hollow in the house. Although Peter waited longer than normal, giving the stooped and arthritic Mrs. Geary plenty of time to make her way to the door, there was no answer. He turned and studied the yard and outbuildings. Deserted.

Peter whistled to Zack and crossed the yard to a path that led to the home of Sam and Mary's eldest son, Seth. The path to Seth's house had grown through the years from a game trail to a rustic sidewalk. Early in their marriage, when the house was newly built, Seth and his wife, Hannah, widened and leveled the trail. They lined it with large river stones and filled-in gravel, and then sand. Every year, each child made a cement handprint steppingstone and placed it along the path. A variety of brightly colored birdhouses, mounted on poles, lined the walk. Wildflowers, roses, and lilac bushes thrived amongst native grasses. At the crest of the hill sat a bench, open on both sides for watching either the sunset or sunrise.

Over the hillcrest in a hidden meadow stood a rambling log house with a garage close behind. Barns and stables filled a distant side yard. Chickens in a variety of colors and breeds pecked for bugs, oblivious to human events. An Australian shepherd puppy, butt wiggling so hard she could hardly walk, slid down the porch steps. Peter stooped to give her a scratch before she wiggled past to greet Zack.

The front screen door squeaked open as Peter climbed the steps. A petite blonde woman, hair tucked into a ball cap, stepped onto the porch.

"Hello, Sheriff. Cows on the road or are you here for cinnamon rolls? I just pulled a fresh batch out of the oven."

Peter laughed. "Thanks, Hannah. I never say no to a cinnamon roll."

Zack and the pup found a gopher hole to inspect so Peter left them to it and followed Hannah into the house. She led him to a sunny kitchen filled with the tantalizing aroma of sugar and cinnamon.

"Sit," she said, pointing to a family sized oak pedestal table surrounded by matching slat back chairs. Peter pulled out a chair to the annoyance of the fat tabby using it for a nap.

"Shoo," said Hannah. The cat yawned and stretched and curled back into a ball.

Peter laughed and pulled out the next chair over. "I know better than to get in a fight with a cat."

"That one's too lazy to do much damage. Would you like coffee with your roll?"

"Tea if you have it." While he waited, he glanced around. "Where's Seth today?"

"He's scouting for elk. We have a few groups of hunters coming this fall. Guiding brings in good money."

Hannah scooped a cinnamon roll dripping with warm butter and icing onto a plate and set it in front of Peter with a fork and a paper towel.

She filled a mug with water from the tap, dipped in a tea bag, and popped it in the microwave. By the time the microwave pinged, a single-serve brewer had a steaming cup of coffee ready. Hannah brought the cups to the table, pushed the tabby to the floor, and sat next to Peter.

"You're not having a cinnamon roll?" asked Peter.

"No way. If I sampled everything I baked, I'd be as big as this table."

Peter took a bite and closed his eyes as he let the flavors melt in his mouth. "This has got to be the best cinnamon roll I've ever tasted."

Hannah blushed. "Thank you. I had to learn how to make them after Sam died. He used to bring us fresh ones from the bakery at least once a week."

"Speaking of Sam, I parked up at the old house. It looked deserted."

"Yeah. Seth's mom didn't do well after Sam died. It's like she lost a part of herself. Physically she was already struggling and then her mind went." Hannah hung her head in shame, eyes welling with tears. "I tried to take care of her here, but it was too much. Even with all the kids in school..."

"She's in the old folks home?"

"Yeah."

"She's in a good place. She has trained professionals taking care of her. You did the right thing."

Hannah looked at him hopefully. "You think so?"

"I know so. I've seen too many neglected old folks. The family means well... or they don't want to spend the money on a home, but, like you said, it's too hard to care for them."

He took a sip of tea. "Speaking of money and old folks, that's why I'm here."

"Um, okay..." Confusion replaced grief.

"There's something strange going on in town. It has to do with antiques. I was hoping you and Seth could help me sort things out."

Hannah nodded. "I think I can clear things up for you."

"Really? I didn't expect it to be that easy."

She laughed. "We've been struggling with the same thing."

"You and Seth?"

"Yeah," she cleared her throat, embarrassed. "Not being a rancher, you probably don't keep up with cattle prices and stuff?"

"I've heard they're down and hay is in short supply."

"Yeah. So, finances are tight for cow/calf operations. Not so bad for us. We need extra hay, but the place is paid for, and dairy prices are good."

"Where do antiques come in?"

"That Fred guy, the one who was murdered... he came around one day and told us he could give us good prices for antiques."

"So, you sold him some?"

"Not right away. We talked about it." She looked embarrassed again. "The thing is... there was a lot of old furniture stored in the sheds and barns... stuff from Seth's parents that nobody really wanted. Furniture was different for that generation. People didn't have much and would never think of throwing it out. They passed it down to their kids. They tried to give it to us when we got married, but... yuck!"

Peter laughed.

"They had this horrible heavy wooden couch upholstered in pink velveteen. It looked like something out of a brothel in a western movie."

"So, you sold it to Fred?"

"That and a lot of other stuff. With Seth's mom in the old folks home, she wasn't around to argue. It cleared up a lot of space we needed for the ranch." She looked up at Peter. "Are we in legal trouble?"

"Not as far as I'm concerned."

"There's more." Hannah swallowed hard. "The day Fred came... Seth got a call from someone wanting to set up a milk account. He had to come back to the house to fill out paperwork. When he got back to the shed, Fred was gone."

Peter sipped his tea, watching emotions ripple across Hannah's face.

"There were things missing that weren't part of the deal," she said.

"Fred robbed you?"

"Yeah."

"You never reported it."

"Seth confronted him. Fred told him that he was part of an antique theft ring and if Seth said anything, we would be implicated." She gave Peter a pleading look. "He said we would go to jail. We've been so worried." She put her head in her hands.

"Hannah... Hannah..."

She lifted her head and wiped tears from her cheeks.

"You've done nothing wrong."

"Really?"

"Yeah, really."

She took a deep breath. "There's another weird thing... that phone call... the one that Seth came back to the house for... it turned out to be a phony business."

"You think Fred had an accomplice? They planned the call to draw Seth away?"

"That's what we think. The phone number, address, everything turned out to be phony."

"Have you talked about this to any of your neigh-bors?"

"Yeah. They're in about the same mess... some of them worse."

"How do you mean?"

"Well... the furniture we sold... it was just old stuff in the barn. I guess you could say it belonged to the ranch. Other folks took stuff... is this confidential?"

"No promises, but I'll do what I can."

She took that in and nodded. "Okay. No names, but I know a guy who sold Fred a grandfather clock from his mom's attic. She's pretty far gone with Alzheimer's and can't get up the stairs anymore. She'll never know the difference. While he was dickering with Fred on the price, someone started honking a car horn down on the road. The guy thinks his horses are out and drives down to take care of things."

"Were the horses out?"

"Nope, and not a car in sight. The guy passed Fred on his way back to the house. Fred just waved and smiled. When the guy got to the house, his mom was crying and said 'the bad man' stole her jewelry."

Peter sighed. "Did that get reported?"

"No. Ten minutes later, she didn't remember Fred being there. Her son brought her to the old folks home the next day. Now he can sell whatever he wants."

Peter rubbed his forehead. Human depravity never ceased to shock him.

"Thanks, Hannah."

WELL-WORN LEATHER CHAIRS sat in front of an ample pine desk in Peter's office, most likely fashioned from local trees for the original Stone County sheriff. A leather sofa lined the far wall under a smattering of vintage western prints.

Settled in, with the office door closed, the crew compared notes.

"Did you get anywhere with the ranchers?" asked Peter.

"Some of them weren't talking, but a few confirmed what we already guessed. Finances are tight so they were selling collectibles and antiques to Fred," said Angus.

"I got the feeling, the ones who wouldn't talk were probably selling them out from under their parents or grandparents and felt guilty," added Helen.

"That's a gray area," said Peter. "Unless there's a complaint of theft, there's no crime to investigate. Family dynamics are complicated. Did any of the ranchers mention Fred stealing from them?"

Helen looked up in surprise. "Yeah. They would be dealing with Fred and get called away. When they came back things were missing."

Peter told them about his conversation with Hannah Geary. "Fred had all these folks running scared after they sold him stuff. For the most part, they're decent people. They didn't dare report him for his theft. They thought they would go to jail."

"It only takes one to be angry enough to kill," said Helen.

"What I don't get," said Angus, "Is where he was putting all those antiques. It wasn't at his house or on the lot full of junk."

"What about Richard Bale?" asked Travis. "It's kind of suspicious he shows up and opens an antique shop while all this is going on."

Peter told them about finding Richard's store unlocked and his conversation with Hobo Joe.

"Could be Bale and Eleanor are going into business together," said Helen. "She has plenty of room in that building. They would save money on rent."

"But were they in cahoots with Fred?"

"When I first interviewed Richard, he said he turned Fred down on a business proposition," said Peter. "But someone is making phone calls for Fred to draw the ranchers away so he can rob them."

"Did you talk to Eleanor?" asked Angus.

"Oh, yeah, she was closed. The note from Thursday about the Women's Club luncheon is still on the door."

"Maybe she's sick. We could do a welfare check."

"Travis, can you find a phone number for her?" asked Peter.

"Sure. What's her last name?"

Blank looks passed around the room. "No idea."

"Uh... does she own or rent that building?" asked Travis.

Again, silence and shrugs.

"There's your project. Find contact information for Eleanor," said Peter. He took the green lanyard out of his pocket and handed it to Travis. "Here's the key in case Richard Bale happens to call asking why we locked his building."

"Have you heard back on the Richard Bale fingerprints?" asked Angus.

"They came up clean."

"Could be he's never been caught."

Travis glanced at his watch. "Birdie should be here by now."

"Did you fill her in on the case?" asked Peter.

"I haven't talked to her. She must have been pretty tired. She hasn't answered her phone all day."

He glanced at his watch again and punched her number into his phone.

"It's going straight to voicemail. She can't be out of service. Her apartment is in town."

⋆

A KNOCK ON the door made Travis jump. He got up and opened it a crack. Debbie, the night dispatcher, grinned at him. "Secret club meeting? I don't know the handshake."

Recently rescued by Peter from the unpleasant position of secretary to Anderson's overbearing and selfish Mayor Kalinski, Debbie was still learning the ropes at the sheriff's office.

Travis forced a smile as he let her into the office. "Hey, Debbie. When's the last time you heard from Birdie?"

She thought for a moment. "I would have to look at the logs for an exact time, but around two this morning."

"Did she say what she was doing?"

"Yeah. She said all the drunks were home safe and she was going home to sleep for a while."

"She had overtime from Fred's house fire," said Peter. "That would be protocol. Did she say anything about turning her phone off?"

"No way. She was still on call, but nothing happened the rest of the night."

Travis bounced nervously on his toes in the doorway.

"Go check on her, Travis. Call as soon as you know anything."

As Travis turned to leave, he stumbled into an elderly white-haired gentleman, Eddie, the bartender for the Roost. "Oops. Sorry Eddie. I didn't see you there," he said, as he grabbed Eddie's shoulders to keep him from falling.

"I've got this, Travis," said Debbie. "You go check on Birdie. What's going on, Eddie?"

"It's Mary. She's missing."

The crew glanced at each other in surprise.

"Oh boy," said Peter. "Bring him in, Debbie."

She led Eddie to a comfortable leather chair in front of Peter's desk and left to answer the phone.

"Why do you think Mary's missing?" asked Angus.

"She didn't come into the Roost all day. I didn't think much about that. She's the boss and keeps her own schedule, but I had a question about a booze order, so I went over to her place." He looked around the room and explained, "She lives in that house out back, you know."

Everyone nodded.

"Her car was parked in the driveway, but she didn't answer her door. I thought that was weird and got worried, so I tried the door. It was unlocked so I went in."

He looked sheepishly around the room at the deputies. "Is that okay?"

"That's just fine, Eddie. What did you find?"

"Her cell phone is lying there on the kitchen table."

"No sign of Mary?"

"No. I looked in all the rooms in case something happened... you know, she was passed out or something."

"Maybe she went for a walk," offered Helen.

Eddie shook his head. "That just doesn't sound like Mary."

He glanced around again for reassurance. "She doesn't go much of anywhere. Drives to the grocery store. Stuff like that."

"Helen," said Peter, "would you go with Eddie and check things out? See if anything looks out of place."

"Sure." Helen stood and led Eddie out the door.

Angus and Peter stared at each other. "Do you sense a pattern?" asked Peter.

"Oh yeah. Richard Bale cleans out most of his shop, leaves it unlocked, and disappears. Birdie isn't answering her phone, and now Mary is missing."

"Hobo Joe saw Richard hauling stuff into Eleanor's shop last night and she's closed today."

"And she didn't take down the note from Thursday."

Peter thought about his interview with Richard Bale the day before, reached into his shirt pocket, and pulled out the business card with Richard's address. He read aloud.

"Aren't those the same apartments where Birdie lives?" asked Angus.

Peter shrugged. "Could be. There's not a lot of rental options in Anderson."

He picked up the phone to call Travis and then changed his mind. Checking on a coworker was one thing. A welfare check on a regular civilian required a deputy.

"Angus, go over there and check out Richard's place and see if Travis found Birdie."

"On it!"

TWENTY MINUTES LATER, Angus, Travis, and Helen were back in the office. Travis was near hysteria. Angus and Helen looked worried.

"She's not at her apartment. Her patrol vehicle isn't there either. We stopped by the Brewery and asked at the food truck. Nobody's seen her," sobbed Travis.

"Nothing is out of place at Mary's, except that she isn't there. Even if she went for a walk around town, it's been way too long," said Helen.

"Did you find Richard Bale?"

"No," said Angus. "He doesn't answer his door and his car is gone. The neighbors say he drives a small white Mazda something or other. They have assigned parking. His slot is empty."

Travis paced back and forth. "We have to find her!"

Peter sat at his desk and rubbed his temples, because he didn't know what else to do. "Debbie!"

"Yes, Sheriff," she said, running into Peter's office.

"Call Tom and see if he's available. We need all the help we can get."

Debbie hurried to her desk and picked up the phone. Short, stout, and balding, Tom Edwards owned the local grocery store. His wife and grown children ran it so well without him, he rarely needed to be there, leaving him available to fill in at the sheriff's office when needed.

"Angus, put out an APB on Birdie and her patrol vehicle."

"On it!"

"Travis!"

Travis continued to pace. Pulling at his hair.

"Travis!"

"Yeah, Boss?"

"Come over here and sit down."

Travis dropped into a chair.

"Listen to me." Peter stared at Travis until their eyes met. "I need you to pull yourself together. Birdie needs you to pull yourself together."

Travis swallowed a sob. "Okay, Boss."

"I'm going to let you ride along with Helen, partly because I don't want you out there on your own. Everyone in this department is going to be searching for Birdie. Understand?"

"Understand."

Angus poked his head in the door. "APB is active."

"Good. Okay, sometime between two a.m. and now, Birdie and her vehicle disappeared. We have no reason to believe she willingly left town. Helen, take Travis and search from Main Street north. Angus, you take from Main south. I'll go east. Debbie?"

"Yes, Sheriff?"

"Did you get ahold of Tom?"

"He's on his way over."

"Great. When he gets here, fill him in and have him search to the west."

Peter stood and whistled to Zack. "Let's go."

21

PITCH BLACK, BUT Mary could see the shadows move. At first the forms were vague, fluid shapes in shades of blacks and grays. As they moved closer, they became more distinct. Murmurs turned to whispers calling her name. Billowing matter and silhouettes transformed into rotted clothing and dry bones.

Mary. Mary. Help us. Save us.

"Why didn't you save me?" pleaded the voice of the long dead Faith.

Birdie awoke to Mary's hysterical screams. Groggy, she pulled herself into a defensive position and gagged on the distinct sour odor of vomit. Her eyes couldn't adjust to zero light. There was only blackness and screams. Screams turned to shrieks of terror, coming from the far side of the room. Birdie wondered why Mary had wandered away from the couch and how she had managed to get so far in the dark.

"Mary!" shouted Birdie, struggling to be heard over Mary's wails.

Shuffling her feet and sweeping front to side with her arms, she inched toward unknown danger.

Mid-scream, Mary's throat gave out, sending her into a coughing fit. She squeezed her pounding head, sure it was going to explode, and puked on the feet of the ghouls. Then they were gone, and she was left once more, alone, in the dark.

Total darkness in an insulated room heightened Birdie's sense of hearing. She followed Mary's soft mews until she bumped into something soft.

"Mary?" Birdie reached down and felt Mary's coarse gray hair. *Wet with sweat or vomit... or blood?*

Birdie dropped to her knees, ignoring the squish and feel of something moist seeping through her pant legs.

"Mary? What happened?" She wrapped a comforting arm around Mary's trembling form, only to be pushed away. More shrieks of terror as Mary's throat recovered.

In spite of the din, Birdie's mind began to clear. *What's going on with Mary?*

She thought back to earlier when they settled on the couch together. Birdie remembered being hungry.

Mary talked about the lost girls in the cave... and she needed a drink. A drink. *Could this be alcohol withdrawal?* Birdie tried to remember her days of heavy drinking. DTs. The secret fear of all drunks. Hallucinations happened in the final phase. *People die of this.*

Knowing better than to touch Mary, who was clearly out of her mind, Birdie sat on the cold floor and thought. She had no way of knowing the time or how long they had been in the room. The air felt heavy. Her head pounded and her wrist ached. She wanted to go to sleep.

It must be daylight by now. Is anyone looking?

Will we suffocate before they find us?

Birdie crawled forward until she found a wall. Protecting her broken wrist and blocking out the pain, she took out her billy club and began a slow tap... tap... tap.

22

Unless it was hidden in a garage, Birdie's patrol vehicle wasn't in the south section of Anderson. Angus drove every street, alley, and dead end. It wasn't there. He headed outward, checking driveways and dirt roads. And then he saw it, a flash of familiar shiny white metal in a grove of cottonwood trees. The trees grew in the ditch next to a county backroad that led to Rumsey, well-traveled and the route home for many ranchers. Whoever dumped the vehicle wasn't local or was in a hurry.

Angus's stomach clenched. Finding bodies in a small community was always difficult. Chances are it would be someone you knew. The possibility that he would find Birdie's body in that vehicle made him nauseous… but she might be alive. Not wanting the news to go over the police radio, he called Peter's cellphone.

"Yeah, Angus."

"I think I found her."

"Is she alive?"

"Don't know yet. I'm almost there. I can see the back of her vehicle hidden in some cottonwoods." He gave Peter his location.

"Proceed with caution. I'll be there in a jif. Angus…"

"Yeah, Boss?"

"Keep this between us until we know what we have."

"Got it."

Angus pulled up to the vehicle and verified it was Birdie's Explorer. He took a deep breath, climbed out of his Explorer, and forced himself forward until he was at Birdie's driver's side window. Empty. He checked the back seat and cargo area. All empty.

He punched in Peter's number.

"Yeah, Angus."

"It's empty, Boss. She's not here."

Peter felt a mixture of relief and fear. *Where is she?* "Okay, call Helen and have her process the scene."

"Travis is with her."

"I know. Helping Helen will give him something to do."

"What now?"

"Meet me back at the office. We'll come up with a plan."

⸻⬥⸻

"HOW'D TRAVIS HANDLE the news?" asked Peter when he and Angus gathered in the office.

"Near hysteria. He had it in his head she was broken down somewhere. He couldn't comprehend an empty vehicle."

"He's in good hands with Helen. She'll take care of him."

"What now?"

"We retrace Birdie's steps. She checked in with Debbie at around two this morning and said all the drunks were home safe. She parks in that same spot every night. All the locals know she's there, but they can't get past her drunk. The tourists don't know any better."

"Okay. Where do we go from there?"

Zack laid his head on Peter's lap and whined.

Peter smiled. "We track her." He looked around. "Do we have anything of hers we can use for scent."

Angus jumped out of his chair. "There's got to be something in her drawer."

He went into the back corner of the outer office where an eight-drawer antique oak file cabinet stood. Each deputy had a personal drawer for storing changes of clothes, toothbrushes, combs and the like. Angus pulled open Birdie's drawer, found a well-worn and much-loved T-shirt and brought it back to Peter's office. Zack instinctively walked over and sniffed the shirt. He looked at Peter.

Peter lifted Zack's trailing harness and thirty-foot rolled bull hide lead from a hook behind his desk. He slipped it over Zack's head, fastened the harness, and said, "Let's go."

They took the back stairs out of Peter's office as the closest route down the hill to the place where Birdie liked to park. When they got to the spot, Peter gave Zack another good sniff of the shirt and allowed him to snuffle unfettered around the area. Trailing differs from tracking in that dogs follow scents in the air rather than on the ground where they can disappear more quickly. Zack stuck his nose in the air, took a few deep sniffs, looked at Peter and waited for the order.

"Find," commanded Peter, and Zack took off down the hill.

He stopped momentarily in front of Eleanor's Tea Parlor, sniffed the air, and then continued on. A turn at the next side street led into the alley going back the direction they came.

Trotting behind, Peter and Angus had the same thought, *this can't be good.*

Zack didn't follow the path of Birdie's vehicle, so she separated from it before it was dumped. They braced themselves for an unpleasant scene but were surprised when Zack stopped at the back door to Eleanor's.

"How accurate is his sniffer?" asked Angus.

"I would trust it with my life. We need to get in there now."

Angus tried the door. Locked.

Peter studied the lock and door frame. "It's a simple knob lock. Not even a dead bolt."

"A crow bar would do it."

"But we don't have one."

"Shoot the lock?"

"We don't know where Birdie is. She could be on the other side."

"That leaves kicking it down."

"The frame wood is as old as the building. Should be easy." Peter, the larger of the men, backed up and put his foot and weight into the inside of the knob. The wood around the lock splintered and the door swung open into a hallway filled with old furniture and boxes.

Peter gave Zack another sniff of Birdie's shirt. "Find."

Halfway down the hallway, they found a door locked with a padlock. Zack sniffed and sat. He focused on the door and whined.

Peter looked around in frustration. There was no kicking down a padlocked door and there were no tools in a tea parlor. "Where can we get a crow bar fast?"

Angus was already out the door and running down the street to the hardware store. He burst through the door and ran past a surprised clerk at the counter, heading toward the aisle where he knew he would find bolt cutters. Grabbing the first one he saw, he turned and ran back out, shouting as he did, "I'll be back to pay for this."

"Sure, Angus," said the clerk to his disappearing form.

Angus found Peter pacing the hallway as panicked as Angus had ever seen him. "This used to be a butcher shop. I'm guessing this was a walk-in freezer room. Even if it isn't cold, it's still air tight. She could be suffocating."

Angus hurried to the locked door, clamped the bolt cutters around the closed shackle of the padlock, and broke it open. Peter flipped the base of the lock, pulled it free and opened the door.

Birdie's body fell out onto the floor.

23

THE HARD FLOOR against her broken wrist woke Birdie. She cried out in pain but was too stiff and drowsy to move.

Angus called an ambulance while Peter helped Birdie into a sitting position.

"Where are you hurt?"

She pointed to her broken wrist with the other hand. "Good to see you," she mumbled.

Peter took off his jacket and wrapped it around her. Zack lay by her side.

"Who locked you in there?"

"Don't know. After Mary—Mary! You have to help Mary!"

"Mary? Mary from the Roost? Where is she?" asked Peter.

"In the room."

Peter turned. "That room?"

"Yeah."

Angus ran his hand along the wall outside the door of the freezer room and found a switch. It took a moment for his eyes to adjust to the bright fluorescent lights. Not far into the room, he found Mary's crumpled body.

"She's here."

"Is she okay?"

Angus knelt next to Mary and felt for a pulse.

"Is she okay?" asked Peter, again.

"Don't think so."

"Alive?"

"Yeah, but not okay."

With fresh air, Birdie's mind began to clear. "She was going into alcohol withdrawal. I thought she died." And she began to cry.

Angus took off his jacket, wrapped it around Mary and waited.

Flashing red lights lit the hallway. Vehicle doors opened and closed. EMT Scott Haugen came through the door followed by ambulance driver Julie Little. They headed for Birdie, but she pointed them into the freezer room.

"I'm okay. She needs you."

They split, with Julie assessing Birdie. Peter led Scott to Mary.

Scott knelt next to Mary and took her vitals while Angus and Peter retrieved the gurney from the ambulance.

When they returned, Scott asked, "So, what's the story here?"

"She and Birdie have been locked in this room since at least early this morning. Birdie mentioned DTs."

"Alcohol withdrawal."

"Yep."

"Makes sense. Pulse fast, breathing shallow, blood pressure high."

"Is she going to make it?"

Scott shrugged. He and Peter lifted Mary onto the gurney, trading Angus's jacket for a warm blanket.

"Any idea how long it's been since she's had a drink?" asked Scott when they stopped next to Birdie in the hallway.

Birdie looked at Peter. "What day is it?"

"Saturday. You checked in with Debbie around two this morning."

"We got locked in not long after that. What time is it now?"

Peter looked at his watch. "Seven thirty-eight. At night." He counted the hours in his head. "You've been in there almost eighteen hours."

"Well, it's been at least that long. She didn't have anything when she showed up."

They watched as the EMTs loaded Mary into the rear of the ambulance.

"Could you guys give Birdie a ride to the hospital?" asked Peter. "We walked down the hill. I don't think she's up to a walk."

"Sure thing," Julie opened the passenger door and helped Birdie get seated and buckled in. "No worries. We'll take care of her."

"What now?" asked Angus as the ambulance tail lights bounced down the alley.

"We search the building. Whoever locked them in there is most likely long gone, but there may be other victims... particularly Eleanor."

Peter's phone pinged. Helen. A ripple of guilt passed across his mind. He should have called, but they'd been busy.

"Hey, Helen."

"We finished processing Birdie's vehicle. Any leads on her whereabouts?"

"We found her. She's alive."

"What?! Where?!" She turned to Travis. "They found her. Alive."

Peter could hear Travis sobbing with relief in the background.

"She was locked in a back room inside Eleanor's Tea Parlor. Did you call to have Birdie's vehicle towed?"

"No need for a tow. They left the keys in the ignition."

"That's handy. Okay, have Travis drive it into town."

"He wants to know where Birdie is."

"On her way to the hospital. In the ambulance... tell him she's okay, just getting checked out."

⸻ ❖◆❖ ⸻

WHILE PETER SPOKE with Helen, Angus inspected the rest of the building. The hallway opened into a dining room filled with round tables covered in pale pink cloths. Dying flowers drooped in vases at the center of each table. A refrigerator motor hummed, and a faucet dripped. Angus breathed deeply, expecting the comforting scents of baked bread, a brewed coffee, but any lingering odors had been replaced by fresh air blowing in through the open back door.

To Angus's eye, other than the wilting flowers, Eleanor had closed up shop as she would any other day. He walked through the small kitchen and the remaining two sales rooms, one filled with used books and the other a sort of gift shop. Neither one showed signs of struggle. Everything in its place. Nothing to see here.

Angus found a dark stairway in the back of the gift shop cordoned off with a 'Private Entrance' sign.

He flipped a light switch, casting a welcoming glow on the steps, and unfastened the clasp holding the cord to the wall.

"Sheriff's department," he called into empty air. No answer.

The landing at the top of the stairs was decorated with a plant in a pot, a reading chair upholstered in a floral pattern, and a wicker basket full of magazines. A sign on the door reminded anyone who had ignored the sign at the bottom of the stairs that this was a private apartment. The door looked like solid wood in a sturdy frame. There would be no kicking in that door. Angus felt for the skeleton key set in his duty vest, but first tried the knob. Unlocked.

"Sheriff's department," he called again as he pushed the door inward. No answer.

Eleanor's apartment smelled of lavender and lemon. Inside, Angus found a living room opening into a kitchen on one side and a hallway to the other. Rooms off the hallway consisted of a feminine bedroom decorated in flowers and frills and an office. All were tidy. No sign of an altercation. No Eleanor.

Angus made his way down the stairs and met Peter at the back door.

"Find anything?" asked Peter.

"Nope. No signs of struggle. No Eleanor."

Peter whistled to Zack. They locked and closed the door, and hurried up the hill to the sheriff's office with Birdie and Mary on their minds.

⋯⋯

PHIL MEYERS STOOD in a dark empty room on the third floor of the Clara Hotel. In spite of the lack of heat in the room and an autumn chill in the air, sweat beaded and dripped down the middle of his back, a sulfurous nervous sweat. He watched as EMTs loaded someone into the back of the ambulance. The sheriff and two deputies were involved. He thought of the back room of Eleanor's shop. The backroom full of stolen antiques. *Do they know?*

He only needed a little more time. A little more time to pull things together, and now everything was falling apart.

24

MARY HAD NO known next of kin, so Dr. Hamm allowed Peter, and Eddie the bartender, to keep vigil at her bedside in the emergency room.

The stillness of her pale, withered body was countered by the many wires, tubes and monitors blinking and humming around her.

A rhythmic gush of air pushed through ventilator tubing going into Mary's lungs, followed by a pause allowing her body to exhale.

"What're her chances, Doc?" asked Eddie.

"As an alcoholic, she's not in good health to begin with. Add a lifetime of cigarettes..." He shrugged.

"You reversed the DTs, though, right?" asked Peter.

"We're treating her with benzodiazepines as a sedative. She's receiving a vitamin and mineral solution through her IV. That and time and rest is the best we can do. Her situation is complicated because of the carbon dioxide poisoning."

"Carbon dioxide poisoning? Like when people have a faulty heater?"

Doc rubbed his tired eyes. "No, that's carbon monoxide. The room Birdie and Mary were trapped in was originally a walk-in freezer for a butcher shop. Air tight." He glanced at the other men. "They're lucky it's such a big room. Half that size and they probably wouldn't have made it out."

"They would have suffocated?"

"It's not so much about oxygen running out as it is about excess carbon dioxide accumulating. Every time you breathe in oxygen, you exhale carbon dioxide. In a room without ventilation, eventually the concentration of carbon dioxide will build to a toxic level."

"So, Birdie has carbon dioxide poisoning, too?" asked Peter.

"A mild case. She'll be headachy and tired for a few days." He looked pointedly at Peter. "I suggest you give her time off."

"Already done. She can't work with that broken wrist anyway. But why is Mary so much worse?"

"She went into shock from of a combination of DTs and carbon dioxide poisoning. Her body couldn't compensate for either condition. Her lungs, kidneys, liver, and probably heart took a beating because of their compromised state… because of her alcoholism and smoking. We intubated her as soon as she came in to regulate her breathing and bring her carbon dioxide level down to normal. But all of this has been hard on her body. She's in a coma."

"A coma?" Eddie's voice took on a panicked tone. "Will she come out of it?"

Dr. Hamm gave his arm a gentle squeeze. "She has a fairly good chance. We won't keep her here, of course. She'll be going to the intensive care unit in Missoula. They're better equipped to handle her condition."

Eddie began to pace. "What're we waiting for? Why is she still here?"

"We've stabilized her, Eddie. She's not in any danger. Life Flight is busy with a multi-vehicle pile-up over by Ronan. It'll be a couple hours before they can get here."

"Can't the ambulance take her?" asked Peter. "They could have her in Missoula in an hour."

"No, not with the amount of equipment she needs. Life Flight is better."

⚊⚊•❀•⚊⚊

TRAVIS DROVE BIRDIE home. Painkillers and the aftereffects of carbon dioxide poisoning made her drowsy so he helped her out of her seat, being careful not to jostle the splint on her arm. He walked with her up the sidewalk to her apartment.

"Are you okay on your own?" he asked at the door.

"I'm good, Travis. No worries. I'll go straight to bed."

"Your wrist isn't too painful?"

"I'm numb from the painkillers... and I'm so tired." She opened her door and stepped in. "See you, Travis. Tell Peter I'll talk to him tomorrow."

Travis waited for the door to close and listened for the sound of the deadbolt sliding into place. Too many people in Anderson left their doors unlocked at night and their car keys in the ignition. Old-time trust. But the world wasn't as safe as it used to be, and Travis wouldn't sleep if he didn't know Birdie was safe. He forced himself to turn away and drive home.

25

W ORD OF THE rescue of Mary and Birdie spread like wildfire around town. Mavis and the mayor, regardless of their possible involvement in the antique gambit, couldn't resist the opportunity for publicity. Peter and his deputies dragged their weary bodies to work on Sunday morning, only to be accosted by an impromptu press conference on the front steps of the court house. Mayor Kalinski primped in a handheld pocket mirror while Mavis answered questions from a KRUD TV crew out of Missoula.

Peter ushered his crew through the crowd to the front doors saying, "No comment," to the reporters as he passed. Mavis, in a stylish pantsuit and sassy curls, shoved a microphone in his face, which he gently removed from her hand, ignoring her protests. He guided her into the building, trailing the microphone cord, which he unplugged from an extension cord inside the door.

In the sheriff's office, Travis opened the bottom drawer of the oak file cabinet and watched as Peter dropped the microphone onto a growing pile. "We're going to have to find a bigger place to store those."

Peter pointed to his office door. "Conference."

The crew and Mavis followed.

"Does this mean I get an exclusive?" asked Mavis as she pulled a tiny recorder out of her shoulder bag.

"No!" said Peter and his crew in unison. Peter held out his hand and Mavis reluctantly handed him the recorder. He verified it was switched off.

"What am I doing here then?" grumbled Mavis.

"Tell us what you know about Fred and the antique business."

Mavis blushed. "What makes you think I know anything about all that?"

"You haven't been hounding us for information."

Silence.

"If you know something, you need to tell us," said Peter.

Mavis rolled a pinky ring nervously as she gathered her thoughts. "It's silly, really. I heard Fred was buying antiques and giving a good price." She couldn't quite meet Peter's eyes. "My mom can't afford to buy food or medication, but she sits in a house full of stuff she doesn't need."

"So, you took things out of your mother's house and sold them to Fred?" prompted Peter.

"Just stuff that she would never miss." Mavis looked at Peter. "I used the money to buy things she needed."

"What about the mayor?" asked Angus.

Mavis nodded. "Yeah. Same thing. Then we heard rumors that he was buying stolen goods. We were so embarrassed. I mean… dealing with someone like that."

"Thank you for your help, Mavis," said Peter. He handed back her recorder.

"This is just between us, right, Peter?"

"Yes, Mavis."

Travis let her out and made sure she left before closing the door.

With everyone seated, Peter studied his crew and sighed. Hardworking, dedicated. *In over their heads?* "We've added two attempted murders and assault of a police officer to our list and still no answers."

"Is Mary going to make it?" asked Helen.

"No idea. Doc says it's too early to tell. They flew her to Missoula last night. She's in the intensive care unit at St. Pat's."

"Word on the street is that she's in a coma."

"Yep."

Angus asked the question that was on everyone's mind, "What was she doing in that room with Birdie?"

"No idea about that either. Mary can't tell us anything at this point. I need to get a statement from Birdie."

No one said the obvious. If Birdie put a civilian in danger, her days as a deputy were over. Travis studied the floor, torn between his feelings for Birdie and resentment for how easily she would throw away her position.

"Don't jump to conclusions. Let's wait and see what she has to say," said Peter. "We had a busy day yesterday. Does anyone have anything new to add?"

"Birdie's Explorer was wiped down, but we found fingerprints on the frame of the rearview mirror," said Helen.

"They always forget the mirror," said Travis. "They adjust it to drive and don't think about it."

"You were able to separate the prints from Birdie's?" asked Peter.

"Yeah. I'm guessing these were from a guy. They're lot bigger and touched a different place on the mirror. We keep a record of employee prints on file, so it was easy to rule out any of us."

Travis stood and headed for the door. "We sent the prints into IAFIS. I'll check and see if they got a hit yet."

"Anything else?" asked Peter, while they waited.

"What about Eleanor?" asked Helen. "She could be another victim. Maybe she witnessed something. Whoever murdered Fred—"

"Her back room is full of antiques that she doesn't sell in her store, but those could belong to Richard Bale. Birdie and Mary were locked in her storage room," Peter shrugged.

"You think Eleanor's involved with Fred and the antique theft ring?" asked Angus.

"I think we need to find her and ask a few questions."

Peter picked up his phone receiver and hit the quick dial button for Judge Knowles. The judge, knowing Peter's number, answered on first ring.

"Mornin', Peter."

"Mornin', Judge. I need a search warrant for Eleanor's Tea Parlor and her private apartment upstairs."

"I have this conversation recorded, of course. Reason for the warrant?"

"Probable cause. We have reason to believe we'll find information necessary to the investigation into the unlawful imprisonment of Deputy Birdie Bradshaw and Mary... uh, Mary of Rustler's Roost."

"Eleanor isn't allowing a search?"

"Eleanor's location is unknown." Peter explained about the note on the door. "At this point we don't know if she's involved."

"You have no way to contact her?"

"We don't even know her last name."

"Consider the warrant electronically signed. Send the appropriate paperwork down when you get a chance."

"Thanks, Judge." Peter disconnected. "Travis, call Tom and ask if he's available for patrol duty."

"On it, Boss," said Travis. He stood and left to make the call.

"Angus, head over and start the search at Eleanor's."

"Sure, Boss," said Angus as he headed out the door.

"Helen, call Birdie and let her know you're on your way over to pick her up. She needs to make a statement."

"I could take a statement at her place... so she doesn't have to come to the office."

"I need to talk to her." Peter ignored Helen's questioning look.

Helen nodded and left Peter alone with his thoughts. Sensing Peter's brooding mood, Travis tapped lightly at the office door.

"Yes, Travis?"

"Tom is on his way. He'll take patrol as long as we need him."

"Great." Peter glanced up after a moment, sensing Travis standing in the doorway. "Something else?"

Travis couldn't suppress a grin. "We got a hit on those fingerprints from Birdie's Explorer."

Peter perked up. "Really?"

"Yeah. Joshua James Green." He handed Peter a paper with photo and information printed off from IAFIS.

"Alias?"

"No. I ran him through the national crime database. He has a few misdemeanors. Petty theft, possession of stolen property, that sort of thing. All in North Carolina. No felony charges."

"Well, that's a start."

"More than a start. I contacted the North Carolina DMV and got his vehicle registration." Travis handed Peter another printed page. "He owns a fourteen-foot Chevy 3500 box truck. That fits the tracks in the alleys behind Eleanor's and the antique store."

"Good work. License plate number?"

"On the registration."

"I don't think we're paying you enough."

Travis laughed, "No argument here."

"Put out a nationwide APB. Add descriptions for Richard Bale and his car. He may be with them."

"On it, Boss." He turned to leave.

"Oh, and Travis..."

"Yeah, Boss?"

"We need a last name and any other information you can find on Eleanor."

"On it."

TRAVIS HAD NO sooner left than Birdie walked in the door, pale and shaky. She sunk into a chair in front of Peter's desk. "Sorry, I guess I'm still recovering. I tried to get by without the painkillers. Bad idea."

"We need to have a serious conversation. Are you up to it?"

"Yeah. I took a pill before we left my apartment. It should kick in soon."

"Good. Tell me what happened Friday night."

Birdie swallowed hard. "Do I still have a job?"

"Just tell me what happened."

"I was on my way home and that delivery truck was blocking the alley."

"Did you happen to get a license plate number?"

"Uh... no. Nothing looked suspicious. I really just wanted to bum some day-old bakery stuff from Eleanor for breakfast and waste time so I wouldn't have to back all the way out the alley."

"You didn't think to call the stop in to Debbie?"

"It wasn't a work stop. I was already called off."

"Okay, where did Mary come in?"

"Not until later, Peter. Honest. I was already in that back room, and I heard someone calling my name. The door slammed shut and everything went dark."

"So, Mary wasn't with you and as far as you know, she didn't know where you were?"

"No. I stopped by her place earlier... after the fire at Fred's. I thought she might have heard something at the Roost that could help us in the investigation."

"How did that go?"

"She said she didn't know anything... and even if she did, she couldn't narc on any of her customers."

"How did she find you at Eleanor's?"

"I don't know. I didn't ask. She said she changed her mind and wanted to help."

"Okay." Peter breathed a sigh of relief. Birdie couldn't be held responsible for a civilian tracking her down. "Do you have any idea who shut the door?"

"No. I heard Mary and then male voices and then the door slammed shut."

"Male voices for sure. You didn't hear a female?"

"Only Mary."

"Did you recognize any of the voices?"

"No."

"Why did you go in that room if you were looking for baked goods?"

"Well... I guess my cop instincts took over. There were all these boxes and old furniture and stuff stacked in the hallway like they'd just been dropped off by the truck. But it wasn't the kind of stuff Eleanor would have in her shop. Something didn't seem right. Then there was that room with all the other antiques." Birdie dropped her head. "I started snooping. I should have called in at that point."

"How long were you in the room before you heard Mary call your name?"

"A few minutes at most. Then I heard her calling, except I thought it was Eleanor. I started toward the door and tripped over a big metal sign and the door slammed and we were in the dark."

"You didn't try to call for help?"

"I did, but the signal was blocked. That room is solid steel."

"So, I've been told." He studied Birdie. *How well do we really know her?* "You didn't know Eleanor was gone?"

"She's gone? Where is she?"

"Not sure. Do you know anything about her? Where she's from, her last name?"

"Uh... no. I've only been in the Tea Parlor a few times, grabbing a sandwich for lunch or a used book. We chatted a little... our favorite authors, that sort of thing."

"But you felt comfortable stopping in the alley in the middle of the night to ask for day old cookies?"

Birdie blushed, giving a hint of color to her pale face. "When you put it that way, it sounds weird." She shrugged. "I was overtired and hungry, and a bag of stale cookies sounded wonderful... Is Mary going to be okay?"

"Don't know. Doc says it's too soon to tell." Peter watched a tear slide down Birdie's cheek. "There's nothing you could have done."

She nodded.

"Go home and get some rest. We won't expect you back until Doc releases you to work." He called to Helen in the other room.

"Yeah?"

"Birdie's ready to go home. After you drop her off, you can go over and help Angus at Eleanor's."

When they were gone, Travis poked his head in the doorway, forehead creased with worry. Peter smiled. "She's clear. Mary went into that building all on her own. Birdie had nothing to do with it."

26

IN A MISGUIDED attempt to avoid unnecessary contact with law enforcement, Richard led the two hooligans in the box truck away from Interstate 15. Instead, they followed Highway 93 through Montana's southwest border, bisected Idaho's boot, and continued into Nevada. Richard's plan was to go south to Ely and then west along Highway 50, known as, "The Loneliest Highway in America." Hundreds of miles of sagebrush and tumbleweeds put Highway 93 in close competition with Nevada's Highway 50 and what better way to avoid attention. The monotonous scenery combined with lack of sleep, had hooligan number two, Logan Jones, struggling to stay awake while his counterpart, Joshua Green, snored in the passenger seat.

Tiny McGill, Nevada would have been a forgettable blip on the highway if not for a set of poor fitting dentures, and Sunday night football.

An elderly patron of Marie's Café in McGill turned to flush after using the facilities, got a tickle in his nose, and sneezed. This caused the upper plate of his dentures to fly out of his mouth into rapidly swirling toilet water, and down the drain. The call to Henry, the plumber, consisted of two panicked voices. One, the hostess frantically trying to keep overflowing water from the plugged toilet out of the dining area, and the other, the owner of the denture plate, worried about his wife finding out he'd lost yet another set of dentures. Henry agreed to drive from his home in Ely on a Sunday, only because the hostess had promised him a double order of smoked ribs and homemade fries, on the house, along with his regular pay.

Toilet unclogged and dentures returned to their grateful owner, Henry collected his tools, a bag of ribs, and a large Styrofoam cup of hot coffee with extra cream and sugar. He said his goodbyes and went out to his utility truck. The ribs were too tempting to wait until he got home, so he set his toolbox and coffee on top of the side bin on the outside of his truck. Leaning against the door he opened the food bag and pulled out the top rib. Mid-chew, he felt a tugging at his pant leg. Neighborhood dogs were not immune to the wafting scent of smoked ribs. A fat white chihuahua, tongue in full drool, stretched as far as possible up Henry's pant leg and whined. A large black lab rounded the corner at the end of the block and headed his way. Henry dropped the rib back into the bag, ran around, and jumped into his driver's seat. The ribs would have to wait. He pulled into the road leading to Ely and home.

Henry's main reason for agreeing to the job in McGill was the promise of ribs and fries to enjoy while he watched his favorite team play Sunday night football. If he didn't hurry, he would miss kickoff. On the road directly in front of him was a white box truck traveling five miles per hour under the speed limit. Logan Jones and Joshua Green were in the truck and had been threatened with their very lives if they got pulled over for speeding.

Henry's patience lasted until just past the edge of town when the box truck showed no signs of picking up speed. He pulled out and stomped on the gas to pass the box truck. As he came around the side of the truck, he hit a pothole. The cup of coffee flew off his side bin and splashed across the box truck's windshield, successfully blocking Logan's view. An even larger pothole caused the forgotten toolbox to bounce and follow the coffee, shattering the windshield. Logan slammed on the brakes and put the truck into park. He and Josh sat, stunned, while Henry, oblivious to the accident he had caused, continued on his way.

Driving behind Henry and his utility truck, Richard Bale watched the entire episode unfold. He pulled his car to the side of the road, jumped out, and ran to the now open window of the box truck.

"What are you doing?! Get out of the road!"

Logan, still in shock, pointed at the shattered windshield. "I can't see."

Richard pointed at Josh. "He can watch out his window and guide you. We can't let the cops get involved."

Truck safely to the edge of the road, Richard used his phone to search for a tow truck. The nearest available was in Ely, twelve miles down the road.

At least it's in the right direction.

He made the call and was assured the tow truck would be there within the hour. A nervous hour. Richard had the guys get out of their truck and lean casually against his car. *Three good 'ol boys chatting it up at the side of the road. Nothing to see here, Officer.*

⚬⚬❖⚬⚬

RICHARD'S ELATION AT reaching Ely later that evening was short-lived. The tow-truck driver deposited the box truck at an auto glass repair shop, pointed out that it was closed on Sundays, and laughed when Richard asked if they would be able to replace the windshield the next day.

"A regular car, maybe, but a big truck like that? That's a special order. Probably a couple days just to get the glass delivered."

He pointed them to the Hotel Nevada. "Cheap rooms, good food, and booze."

Richard considered his options. His first instinct was to cut and run. Nothing wrong with his car. His second thought was the inventory in the truck, most importantly, the value. That load would salvage his island retreat retirement plans. Walking away... he didn't want to think about it. What he really needed was sleep. One night wouldn't make a difference. His mind would be clearer in the morning.

The Hotel Nevada held down a corner of a city block saturated with neon. That should have been Richard's first subtle hint of trouble. Seeing Josh's eyes light up in the motel lobby knocked the point home. Gambling machines blinking as far as the eye could see coupled with old-time décor—guns, branding irons, and mounted game heads—had him swaggering like a cowboy. Free coupons for margaritas on check-in sealed the deal.

Richard should have turned around and found a motor inn on the edge of town, his mistake. He paid for a room for Logan and Josh, not out of generosity, but to ensure they went to a room. He pocketed the free drink coupons and walked them upstairs.

Having driven the bulk of the distance from Anderson, Logan's only thoughts were dinner, something fast and filling, and bed. Josh, having slept most of the drive, was ready for action. His brief trips out west consisted of dropping off a load of stolen antiques and picking up another. East to west and west to east.

"Come on, Logan. Let's go down for one drink. What could it hurt?"

"You heard him. He said stay in our rooms. Who knows what he'll do if he catches us out."

"What can he do? We're grown men."

"He won't pay us for the trip for one thing... and I'm bushed anyway." Logan picked up the phone and hit the button for room service.

"Two deluxe burgers with fries," he said when the hostess answered. He noticed Josh's frown. "And a couple a' beers... whatever you have on tap."

He has to go to sleep sometime, thought Josh. He settled on his bed and turned on the television.

Logan fell asleep halfway through his burger. Josh finished both beers, felt the buzz, and slipped out of the room. *Party time.*

27

"Y OU WANNA' GO on a stakeout?"

Surprised, Dixie paused. "Gee, Peter, are you hoping I'll bring food or is this your idea of a fun date?"

"Think of it as dutch. You bring the food, I'll provide entertainment."

"Is this going to be like those stakeouts on TV where I have to pee in a jug?"

Peter laughed. "You can have as many potty breaks as you need."

"I had planned to stay home and scrub the grout in the shower, but, hey, I'll make the sacrifice for you. Is Zack going to be there?"

"No. Not fair to keep him shut up in the truck for hours."

"Okay. You can bring his food home for later. When and where?"

"I'll pick you up tonight at seven and explain everything."

"Sounds good. See you then." She disconnected.

Travis stuck his head into Peter's office. "I have some interesting info on Eleanor."

"Do tell," said Peter, swinging his feet off his desk.

"I checked with the county clerk. Eleanor doesn't own that building. Her name is nowhere on the title."

"Really? Who owns it?"

"Fred Filmore."

Peter sat for a moment letting that sink in. "So, maybe Eleanor was just renting the space?"

"Who knows. If there was a contract between them, it burned in the fire."

"That could explain the antiques stored in the backroom. His building, his antiques."

<hr>

NEVER HAVING OWNED anything besides the house and meadow he inherited from his mother, Fred was out of his element when it came to real estate. After taking the wrong turn and discovering Anderson, his next step was finding a place to live and a place to store his stolen goods. The real estate offices along Main Street were intimidating. Multi-million-dollar ranches and creek-side mansions. Out of his reach. He walked up one side of the street and down the other. Mid-block past an historic hotel, the Clara, he found a vacant lot and considered. Not ideal, but a possibility. On the other side of the lot stood a two-story brick building with an abandoned air. Shades covered the windows, and a large 'For Sale' sign with a phone number written in black sharpie blocked most of the door glass. Fred shaded his eyes and peered around the edges. Tables and chairs. A display case and cash register. *A restaurant?* That reminded him of his missed breakfast. He got back in the van and drove down the street to the diner.

Dixie's was busy with the breakfast crowd, but Fred found an empty stool.

"Coffee?" asked a tired waitress, setting a menu in front of him.

"Uh... yeah. Hey, lots of people in town. Is it always like this?"

"Always," the waitress sighed. "Sapphire diggers and outdoorsy people in the summer. Hunters in the fall. Skiers in the winter. The Brewery is busy all year." She poured his coffee. "You moving in?"

"Naw. Just curious." Stolen antiques or not, Fred didn't need nosy Nellies getting into his business. He ordered the Farmer's Omelet and began to dream his own dreams.

Fred finished his breakfast, paid his tab, and drove back to the empty building. The streets were busier. The closest parking place he could find was several blocks down a side street. He cursed himself for not calling the phone number the first time he was there. Digging through the glove box, he found a pen and a scrap of paper. Walking was not high on his list, especially up hill. He momentarily reconsidered Montana. He could find somewhere flat to settle. Maybe Kansas. But Kansas wasn't a hot spot for antique dealing and there was something special about this town.

The property owner answered the phone on the first ring, and sounded a tad too eager to find a buyer for the building.

28

Entering through the back of Eleanor's Tea Parlor proved to be easier than expected. The lock, damaged from Peter's kick the day before, barely held the door closed. Angus donned a pair of nitrile gloves from his utility belt and studied the furniture and boxes lining the hallway from the delivery Friday night. The boxes were basic brown cardboard, dirty and well-used, without distinguishing marks. He opened several of them and found an odd assortment of hastily wrapped collectibles.

Looks like someone cleaned out a bunch of old farmhouses.

Angus knew from listening to his mother that many of the items, along with the furniture, were valuable to antique dealers and collectors. A quick walk through the room where they had found Birdie and Mary revealed much of the same. He followed the hallway into the dining room.

Unlike the night before, the air was stagnant and heavy from being closed off in the heat of the day. Angus sniffed. An odor reminiscent of his father's barn after hunting season hung in the air. Only different. Angus knew that smell. Human blood.

Exploring the room, he found no obvious source of the odor so he climbed the stairway to Eleanor's apartment. "Sheriff's department," he called, not expecting an answer.

"Sheriff's department," he called again as he pushed the door inward.

Having walked through the night before, Angus by-passed the rest of the apartment and concentrated on the office. A desktop computer sat on a cherrywood desk flanked by a matching two-drawer file cabinet. Angus opened the file cabinet first. Folders labeled with distributer names filled the top drawer. He rifled through the first few files and found invoices for food and other assorted supplies needed in the running of the tea shop. The bottom drawer held similar folders, but these were focused on the gift and used book sections of Eleanor's business. Nothing in the files hinted at personal information for Eleanor. They were all addressed to Anderson Emporium with the physical address of the tea parlor. Angus closed the drawer and moved to the desk. The desktop was clear except for the usual paraphernalia. Stapler. Tape dispenser. Magnetic paperclip holder. All in a pink and white flowery design. Printed on a pink sticky note stuck to the bottom edge of the computer screen was a random string of letters and numbers.

Computer password?

The irony of Eleanor picking a hard-to-guess password and then sticking it to the computer wasn't lost on Angus. He leaned over, tapped on the keyboard to wake the screen and typed in the code printed on the sticky note.

Bingo!

Angus pulled out the chair in front of the desk, sat, and scooted himself in closer. An array of icons led him into computer files, but instead of enlightenment, he became more confused. Every file was listed under the name of Fred Filmore and every file pertained to the business listed as Anderson Emporium. There were no social media accounts or even an email for Eleanor. Frustrated, Angus pulled open the center desk drawer. Pens, sticky note pads, white-out correction tape. He opened the top of a column of drawers on the right side of the desk. The top drawer contained business envelopes and stamps. The next drawer, extra tape and staples, and the bottom drawer, a ream of copy paper. Baffled, Angus left the office and did a more thorough search of the rest of the apartment. The bedside table held a few romance novels and a book light. He opened the closet. He couldn't tell if there were clothes missing. The bulk of the hangers and shelves were full. Shoes filled a line of clear boxes along the back wall.

"Angus?" Helen called his name from below.

"Up here," he hollered as he made his way back through the apartment and down the stairs. He found Helen standing in the middle of the tea room looking puzzled.

"What?" he asked.

"Something isn't right. I was in here last week buying a book and the tables were arranged differently."

"So?"

"So, the way they're arranged now makes no sense. Before, there was a good flow. Now there's that group crowded together in the back and a big space in the middle. Makes no sense. And do you smell blood?"

"Yeah, but I can't find where it's coming from."

"Let's move those tables in the back."

Four Windsor chairs were arranged around each table. Loom rugs were centered underneath, each with a different country scene. Helen and Angus lined the chairs along the wall. Each taking a side, they lifted the tables and moved them closer to the front of the room until the entire rear was empty but for the rugs. Helen walked over to the far rug, stooped, and grabbed onto an edge.

"Well, here goes."

Immediately her nostrils were assaulted with a musty acrid smell. A reddish-brown stain filled most of the space. It had oozed into the dry wooden floor and the wool fibers of the rug. Blood, and lots of it.

"I think we've found our murder scene."

Helen grabbed her crime scene kit sitting by the far wall. "I don't smell bleach, so we'll go with the luminol rather than fluorescein."

"Why's that?" asked Angus, always ready to learn.

"Luminol doesn't work if someone tried to clean with bleach." Helen spritzed luminol around the rug while Angus lowered the shades on the window and shut off the lights.

"Wow!" said Angus as the area around the rug glowed with a blue light.

Helen expanded her spritzing, revealing drag marks and footprints to the back door. "Someone cleaned these marks but gave up and covered the rest with a rug.

"Fred's blood?"

"Could be. We'll take a sample and send it to the crime lab for comparison."

"Who else?"

"Well... Eleanor is missing."

"In more ways than one."

"What do you mean?"

"Upstairs. It's weird. She lives there... her clothes and stuff are there, but..."

"But what?"

"But there aren't any papers... personal letters... nothing that has her name on it. She doesn't even have a social media account. Everything is under Fred's name."

"Weird."

"Yeah."

While Helen processed the scene below, Angus went back upstairs. He packed the desk computer and contents of the file cabinet into evidence boxes and loaded them into his Explorer. After securing the area with yellow crime scene tape, he went in to check on Helen.

"All done?" he asked.

Helen was leaning, tired, against a wall. "Yeah, I'm bushed. Peter called. I told him about the blood. He said he's busy tonight and we could go over everything in the morning."

"Peter, busy?"

"Yeah, I know."

Angus thought of Holly and decided to drive by her house on his way home, praying Peter's truck wouldn't be parked in the driveway.

29

WHIRRING, BEEPING, AND jangling lured Josh into the casino. It wasn't a hard hook. It's what he came for. On the lookout for newbies, a waitress followed him with her eyes as he wandered among the slots until one piqued his interest and he sat. He reached into his pocket and pulled out his wallet.

"Hey, handsome, just get to town?"

"Uh... yeah."

"Do you have your free margarita coupon?"

"What? No," he huffed. "Dang Richard took it."

"No worries." She pulled one out of her apron pocket and smiled. "I have an extra."

"Gee, thanks." He gave her what he thought was a charming grin.

"Peach, raspberry, or jalapeno?"

The waitress was young and attractive and Josh, deep in a daydream, gazed blankly into her eyes.

"Sir?"

"Uh... what?"

"What flavor margarita do you want? Peach, raspberry, or jalapeno?"

"Uh..." Josh wasn't fond of jalapenos, but it struck him as the most manly flavor. "Jalapeno. Yeah, definitely jalapeno. I like hot stuff." He gave her a knowing wink.

To her credit, she held her smile and didn't roll her eyes until she turned around. Friendliness equaled tips.

Three margaritas, extra strong, and a hundred dollars gone in the slot, Josh was now more interested in fighting than flirting. He eyed a couple at the next machine and convinced himself the man gave him a dirty look. The man said something to the girl. She laughed, and Josh decided she was definitely laughing at him. That was an invitation for a brawl if he ever saw one, so he stood on wobbly legs, walked over to the man and punched him in the nose as hard as he could. The couple were there with a large wedding party, all of whom were happy to join in the fray. Bedlam ensued.

JOSH WOKE UP the next morning to a shrill alarm. He grabbed his head. Pain. Bleary eyes focused on the bars of a jail cell. *Dang.*

Fortunately for Josh, by the time the sheriff's department had everything under control at the casino, nobody could remember who started the fight. The whole group was thrown into lockup for the night to sober up.

Unfortunately for Josh, his name pinged on an APB out of Montana.

30

EVERYONE IS FAMOUS in a small town, and it was Eddie's time to shine. Sitting at Mary's bedside after her rescue, in the hospital hallways, and fetching coffee from the cafeteria, he listened to conversations. He knew more than he should have about the case and was happy to share. Word spread fast about the room full of antiques in the back of Eleanor's Tea Parlor, a shop that didn't sell antiques. Townsfolk made the connection. Folks who had been robbed by Fred. What they sold to him fair and square was one thing, but they wanted the stolen stuff back and now they knew where to look.

What began as casual dinner conversation at the Silver Dollar Saloon over the whiskey steak special turned into an after-dinner meeting in a nearby barn. Whiskey flowed and tempers flared.

⚬⚬⚬

PETER PULLED UP in front of Dixie's house and sat for a moment wondering if it would be appropriate to honk or if he should go to the door. A date would require going to the door, but this was two old friends on a stakeout.

While he pondered, Dixie watched through a gap in the curtains, confused. She was expecting Peter in his patrol vehicle. Instead, he was sitting there in a metallic blue Chevy Colorado pickup truck. At the same time she opened the door to investigate, Peter opened his door and stepped out, choosing to err on the side of good manners.

"Did you borrow a truck?"

"It's my going to town truck."

"I've never seen it before."

Peter laughed. "Which makes it a perfect stakeout vehicle,"

Dixie reached into the house and grabbed a small cooler before she walked down the sidewalk.

Peter helped her into her seat. "It spends most of the time parked in the garage. I rarely go to town."

After Peter got back in the truck and they both buckled up, Dixie said, "I brought good snacking food that will last us a few hours."

"Good. I'm running on apple cider and pumpkin cookies."

"New diet?"

"No, an old one. It comes from having a sister-in-law who always has cookies on hand."

Hoping Phil wasn't in the habit of checking the area for strange vehicles, Peter parked across the street and down a block, a perfect position for watching Phil's front door and garage.

"So... who are we watching?"

"Phil Meyers."

"The manager of the Clara Hotel?"

"Yeah. He's a suspect in Fred's murder."

"No kidding?"

"Maybe not top of the list, but I'm running out of people to investigate. Richard Bale is a suspect, but he's in the wind. I'm not sure if Eleanor is a suspect or another victim. At any rate, she's nowhere to be found."

"So here we are."

"Here we are. Phil has reason to want Fred dead and he doesn't have a legitimate alibi for the night of the murder. His wife says he comes home, eats dinner, and falls asleep in front of the television. Helen suspects the wife is a drinker and passes out upstairs."

"So, she wouldn't know if he left the house or not."

"Exactly. So, we're going to sit and watch."

"I'm not sure where the 'entertainment' comes in."

"Just wait," Peter smiled. "So, what did you bring to eat?"

"Triple-dipped fried chicken." She opened the cooler. "I wrapped it in aluminum foil so it should still be warm." She handed Peter a foil wrapped package and a bottle of water. "And more snacks for later."

Peter unwrapped two large chicken thighs and a drumstick. The first juicy bite brought him back to his childhood. "This is your mom's recipe."

"She taught me well."

"She and your dad... they made all the difference for us after our parents died."

"I miss them."

"Did it ever bother you? Paul and I being around all the time?"

"Not really. I was daddy's little girl. And he never took you anywhere that I wasn't invited."

"Except Boy Scout campouts."

"Well, except those, but Mom always had something special planned for me."

They chewed and thought and chewed some more, both comfortable in the silence.

"Do you still think about what happened?" asked Dixie.

"To my parents?"

"Yeah."

"I planned on solving their murder someday, but," he took a deep breath and let it out slowly, "I can't get myself to open the murder file. I can't bear to see the pictures of them lying there." He glanced over at her. "Silly, huh?"

"Oh, Peter. Nobody would want to look at that. Why not get someone else to help you? Someone who didn't know your parents?"

Peter thought. "I would have to open up to someone. Tell them the story."

"Peter."

"Yeah?"

"This is a very small town. Everyone knows."

Before he could reply, a whirring sound brought their attention to Phil's house. The garage door rolled open and a dusty maroon four-door sedan backed out and into the street.

"Bingo."

Peter waited until the car was at the end of the block and turning before he started his truck, put it into gear, and followed.

Dixie slid the chicken packet off his lap and stuffed it back into the cooler. She stowed the cooler in the back seat and took a deep breath to steady her nerves. Ready for action.

As they drove, Peter told her the rules. "If things go bad, do NOT get out of this truck unless I tell you to. Okay?"

"Got it."

"Even if you have to use the bathroom..."

"I'll hold it… is that what happened to Mary?"

"Something like that. She saw Birdie's patrol vehicle and went into the building without considering it might be a bad situation."

"I'll stay in the truck."

They followed Phil's car through several turns and then onto a side street off Main. Phil parked at the curb, got out, and cut across a yard filling the space between a small brick bungalow and a business. He stopped, looked both ways, and went through the back door.

"That's Rustler's Roost," said Dixie in surprise. "What would someone like Phil Meyers be doing in the Roost?"

"Good question. Phil's a candy pants compared to the usual clientele."

He unbuckled his seatbelt.

"You're really going in there? Don't you need backup or something?"

"I'm off duty. I'm going in for a relaxing cocktail."

"Uh huh."

"Seriously though, don't get out. Keep the doors locked. I'll leave the keys. If I'm not back in fifteen, drive home. Call dispatch and tell Debbie what's going on."

"Be safe."

Peter locked the truck door on his way out. He went to the back door of the Roost and let himself in.

The door opened into a dim hallway. He could see light at the far end and hear the typical sounds of a bar in full swing. Clinking glasses, raucous laughter, the click of balls on the pool table. There were several closed doors, two on each side of the hallway. Peter guessed Phil wasn't in the bar. If the bar had been his destination, he would have gone in the front door. A square plastic sign with the silhouette of a man hung in the middle of the first door on the right. Men's bathroom. Peter tried the door on the off chance Phil stopped to use the restroom. The door was unlocked and the room empty. Peter tried the door across the hall. It opened into a closet. Mop and broom, cleaning supplies, extra toilet paper. The next door on the right was the ladies room. Running out of options, he put his ear to the door across the hall. Muffled men's voices, the scrape of a chair, a strong odor of cigar smoke. This was it. Peter didn't bother knocking. He opened the door into a room dominated by a large wooden professional poker table. The table was covered in cards and cash and surrounded by men. Several jumped out of their chairs at the sight of Peter, a gut reaction from lifetimes of being on the wrong side of the law. Phil Meyers, on the far side of the table, sat stone still, mouth agape, eyes like saucers.

"Relax. There's no law against playing poker in Montana," said Peter, moving further into the room.

"Uh... so what are you doing here, Sheriff?" asked one of the standing men.

"Saw Phil coming in and remembered something I needed to ask him."

Everyone looked at Phil who continued to sit, ashen faced, sweat beading on his forehead. The men standing, sat, and picked up their cards. The law wasn't after them.

"Can we finish our hand first?" asked one.

"Sure. No hurry." Peter found a spectator chair along the wall, sat and pulled a foot on a knee. Relaxed.

The game continued without much action on Phil's part. In the end, the other men played around him and took whatever he had contributed to the pot.

Peter stood and motioned to Phil. With the demeanor of someone being sent to the principal's office, Phil reluctantly stood and followed.

Outside, Peter gave Dixie and thumbs up. "Let's talk in your car," he said to Phil. "You're not under arrest. I'm just here to ask you questions about our investigation."

Phil nodded, not really listening. He fumbled in his pocket for his car keys and clicked open the locks. He climbed in and, out of habit, buckled his seatbelt while Peter slid into the passenger seat.

"I'll pay it all back, Peter. I promise. Somehow I'll pay it all back," and then he started to cry.

Accustomed to the emotion of regret from crooks who have been caught, Peter sat silent and waited. The tears were short-lived.

Phil stiffened his spine and wiped his face with his sleeve. "What now?"

"Tell me your story and we'll go from there."

He took a deep breath and coughed, hands gripping the steering wheel. Knuckles white. "It was that trip to Vegas that started it all."

"Vegas?"

"Yeah. Pam had a group of friends she would meet at the Brewery now and then. Usually when they had special music. The other girls were planning a weekend trip to Vegas with their husbands and Pam convinced me to go along." He looked at Peter, his eyes pleading for understanding. "I'd never been any place like that. All the lights and people. Add too much booze..."

"What happened?"

"We started out with the slot machines. The other guys kept saying that was sissy ladies' stuff and drug me over to the poker tables. That's where things get blurry. Lights. Crazy music. Booze. I woke up the next day on the bathroom floor. Lying in my own vomit. My head felt like it'd been split open."

"Where was Pam?"

"She was already out of bed and packed... and mad. She wouldn't speak to me. We had to cut the trip short. It wasn't 'til we got home I found out why."

"Why you had to go home early?"

"Yeah." He hung his head in shame. "I lost more money than we had at that poker table. She had to call the bank and transfer what she could from savings to pay our tab. The rest went on credit cards." He began to cry again. "I ruined us."

Peter stayed silent, willing Phil to confess his sins.

"Pam took on a part-time job at the grocery store. That didn't last long. She got fired for going to work drunk. After that, she started selling her paintings in shops around town. Pays for her booze anyway."

Peter waited.

"I had no choice. We couldn't pay the bills. Our credit rating tanked. The bank wouldn't give me a loan."

Peter bit his lips. *What did you do, Phil?*

"I hear a lot standing there at the door of the Clara Hotel. Little bits of conversation... and I see a lot, too."

Silence. Peter waited.

"I found out what Fred was doing... buying antiques from townsfolk who needed extra money. The Clara has so much... so many antiques. Lots of it in storage. I knew nobody would miss them."

"So, you stole antiques from the Clara and sold them to Fred."

"Borrowed. I borrowed them. I was going to replace them when everything straightened out."

Tempting as it was, Peter didn't explain the difference between borrowing and stealing.

"Then Fred found out where I was getting the antiques and threatened to turn me in."

"What did he get out of that?" asked, Peter, breaking his silence.

"He wanted more. More antiques and I had to take less of a cut."

"Good luck for you when he died."

"I didn't kill him!" Phil wiped his sweaty hands on his pants. "I need a lawyer." He said and clamped his mouth closed.

So close.

Peter pulled his phone out and punched in the number for Debbie at dispatch.

"Hi, Peter."

"Hey, Debbie. Who's on duty tonight?"

"Helen until midnight."

"Could you send her over to Rustler's Roost. I'm in a maroon sedan. We're parked along the side street. I have an arrest and transport."

31

After Helen Hauled Phil to jail, Peter found Dixie wrapped in a flannel blanket he kept in the back seat for Zack. The cooler sat beside her on the seat.

"I ate the rest of the chicken." She sneezed and rubbed her nose. "Dog hair."

"I am so sorry. I should have sent you home."

"I had the keys. I could have left."

"I owe you a real date."

"Lady's choice?"

"Anything you want."

"Deal."

They drove around the block and turned east on Main. As they drove past Eleanor's Tea Parlor, Peter noticed lights on inside.

"We'd better check this out."

The street was empty, so he backed up, turned off his headlights, and parked in front of the store.

He punched in the number for dispatch.

"Hi, again. Your second call of the night. I thought you were off duty," said Debbie when she answered.

"Yeah, me too. Hey, is Helen finished processing Phil?"

"Yep. He's all tucked in for the night."

"Send her over to the tea parlor. Tell her to go through the alley and let me know before she gets there."

Out of uniform and missing his required Stetson and patrol vehicle, Peter wasn't immediately recognizable. As he and Dixie sat watching, they could see movement in the back of the building.

"How are you holding up?" asked Peter.

"Cold, tired, and I have to pee."

"As soon as Helen gets here, you take the truck and go home. I'll catch up to you later."

She managed a weak smile.

Peter's phone pinged. Helen.

"I'm ready to go in."

"Which end of the alley?"

"Facing east. Opposite Fred's lot."

"Okay. I'll walk through Fred's. When I give you the signal, lights and sirens full blast." Peter reached across the seat, unlocked the glovebox, and took out a gun. He gave Dixie's shoulder a quick squeeze.

"Are you going to be okay?" she asked.

"No worries. I'll give you a call when I get home." He grabbed his duty vest and belt from the backseat and let himself out.

Dixie scooted across the seat to the driver's side, put the truck into gear, and waved goodbye.

The clutter in Fred's lot had not improved since his death. Peter used the flashlight from his duty vest and did his best to navigate through without making noise. Treading softly, he rounded the corner of the building and saw several men, all in cowboy hats and boots, walking back and forth through the backdoor of Eleanor's, carrying boxes and furniture.

He called Helen. When she answered, he said "Now!"

Lights and sirens erupted from Helen's end of the alley. The group of cowboys stood stock-still, stunned. None of them were seasoned robbers and all too drunk to process clearly. The ones remaining in the building when the siren started poked their heads out the door, rubberneckers looking for the emergency.

There were five of them and Peter recognized every one. Local ranchers. Most likely victims of Fred's thievery.

He strode into the light. "What have you boys got yourselves up to?"

Eventually a wiry, leather-faced cowboy spoke. "We, uh, we was just getting' stuff Fred had stored in here."

"Yeah," murmured a few of his companions. "Our stuff fair and square, Sheriff."

"Besides the fact that you crossed into a crime scene, do you have permission to be in this building?"

The cowboys glanced around at their companions, nonplussed. One attempted bravado. "It's our stuff. We don't need permission to take it."

"You need permission to break into a building that doesn't belong to you," answered Peter.

No answer. Helen was standing in the perimeter. Peter gave her a nod and she began. "You have a right to remain..."

Peter unclipped the handcuffs on his belt. He would have to call Missoula or Anaconda. He didn't have the jail space for all the prisoners of the night.

32

J OSEPH MARSH HATED the smell of blood. He hated the sight of raw butchered animals hanging from hooks. He hated the words 'family business'. Most of all, he hated the building in Anderson. His father was a butcher, as was his grandfather. Generations of Morris men cut, wrapped, and sold countless steaks and chops out of that building. As soon as he could safely weld a knife, Joseph was forced to take his place at the cutting table.

The day he turned eighteen, Joseph said his good-byes, packed his second-hand Toyota, and drove to Missoula. Granted, the only decent paying job he could find was as a butcher in a grocery store, but he only stayed long enough to complete two years of an accounting degree at the university. That education landed him a job as a bookkeeper. Two years and a CPA exam later, he opened his own business and vowed he would never touch another piece of raw meat.

As an only child, Joseph inherited the butcher shop, the adjoining vacant lot, and the decrepit family homestead next to what was now the county landfill. On a sentimental whim, his father stipulated in the will that if Joseph sold the properties, they had to be sold together. It should have been easy to sell property in a thriving tourist town like Anderson, but no bank would finance a mortgage. The butcher shop couldn't pass an inspection and none of the problems were easy fixes. They found asbestos in the insulation, the drywall, and the glue used under the floor tiles. Tree roots were growing through the sewer pipes and the electrical wiring was iffy. "Fire trap" is how one inspector put it.

Joseph's only option was to finance the deal himself with a rent-to-own option. People were the next problem. Tourists visiting Anderson were sucked into romantic dreams of running a business in the charming little town. Those dreams turned to nightmares when they realized how much work and money went into running a business and restoring an old building. A toy store, a travel agent, and, finally, a coffee shop each failed within their first six months of business.

Joseph allowed himself a moment of hope when he received Fred's call. He canceled all appointments and drove as fast as he dared to Anderson.

Fred didn't ask about clogged plumbing, or outdated electricity, or asbestos. He didn't care. He was awed by the amount of space inside the building.

"Looks like it used to be a restaurant," he said as he stood in the front room.

"A coffee shop. They served sandwiches and stuff too. A couple from Washington State. They didn't last long."

"How come?" asked Fred.

Joseph bit his tongue and mentally kicked himself. *Way to scare off a potential buyer.*

"Uh... some sort of family issues. They went back to Washington." He correctly judged that Fred wasn't a high roller. "The property is owner financed. Low interest, of course." He cleared his throat. "Oh... uh... there are other conditions to the sale."

"What conditions?" asked Fred, his dream bubble fading.

"The vacant lot next door and a house. They come as a package deal."

"What kind of house?" Fred saw dollar signs flash before his eyes. No way he could afford all that.

"It's out of town a ways. I'll drive you." Joseph led Fred to a white Jeep Cherokee parked in the vacant lot. "This is a great parking lot for a business," he said, selling hard. "That's a bonus in this town."

Down the highway several miles and a turn onto a gravel road brought the men to the gates of the county landfill. Outside the gates, a potholed dirt track led into a shallow ravine.

"The road's a bit rough, but a grader could smooth it out in a jiffy."

Fred was thinking it would take a couple tons of dirt to fill in the ravine and had no intention of driving that road on a regular basis. Absolutely not was the answer sitting on his tongue until they got to the end of the road. There sat a decrepit clapboard farmhouse dressed in peeling white paint, much like Fred's childhood home. He was hit with a wave of nostalgia and agreed to look inside.

The couple from Washington had cleaned and added a smattering of fresh paint in the short time they were there, but the house was outdated by a century, and dusty from months of standing empty. Fred didn't notice these things. He was thinking of decades of living on the road, cheap motels and shabby rentals. He realized he was weary. The idea of coming home to the same place every night felt good. Home alone. No nagging mother. No disgruntled Eleanor. A house of his own.

"How much?" he asked.

Joseph wisely quoted a monthly payment rather than the total amount. Affordable.

Fred managed a smile. "Okay."

Well prepared, Joseph handed Fred a pen and a stack of papers, required signature lines marked with yellow 'sign here' stickers. He dropped Fred off in town, sealing the deal with a hardy handshake and keys to the building.

Contemplating his plan for the space and thinking back to the waitress at the diner, Fred began to worry. Anderson was a small town and people would talk... and they would watch and wonder what he was doing. He couldn't stay under the radar right there on the busiest part of Main Street. He needed a cover.

He had a wonderful idea. Then he panicked. Eleanor.

<hr>

ALL ELEANOR HAD ever done was work in diners for cash. She had never rented a room or driven a car or had a bill to pay. She worked hard and handed her money over to Fred. Well, most of her money. She'd been skimming off tips for years and lately he was too busy looting and selling to pay attention to her meager wages. When he stopped counting, she stopped giving. She had a nice nest egg of her own built up. Now she found herself without a job. Dixie's wasn't hiring and specifically wasn't interested in paying anyone under the table. The owner, Dixie, had very politely suggested a bar called Rustler's Roost.

Eleanor stood on the sidewalk in front of the Roost, gathering courage, when she heard a squeal of brakes on the road.

"Eleanor!" Fred called from the van. "I've been looking all over for you."

She turned, baffled. He actually sounded happy to see her. "Why?"

Cars started to honk behind the van. "Hurry. Get in," said Fred, remembering to sound like the bully he was.

She grabbed the handle of her suitcase and jogged over to the passenger door, barely managing to pull the suitcase onto her lap before Fred hit the gas and took off. He turned around and headed back up Main Street, but this time he parked in the alley behind his new building.

"The diner's not hiring," said Eleanor.

Fred grunted. He pulled out a set of keys and motioned for her to follow.

Fred didn't like questions so, through the years, Eleanor had learned not to ask. She stepped out of the van, watched as he unlocked the back door, and followed him in. Fred led her through a dark hallway that opened into a spacious room filled with restaurant style dining tables and a serving counter with a display case. Behind the counter, an opening led into a kitchen filled with shiny stainless-steel appliances. Doorways on the far wall of the main area led to two more rooms.

"Here's the deal," began Fred. "You've been a burden to me for years."

Eleanor hung her head, she'd tried so hard.

"I'm setting you free from your obligations," Fred continued. "I took you on as a favor to your father and wouldn't feel right about leaving you with nothing, so I'm going to allow you the use of this building free of charge. Except for the storage area in back, that's mine."

Eleanor couldn't help herself. "Whose building is this?" she asked.

Fred puffed out his flabby chest. "Mine. I bought it this morning."

She stood and blinked. Processing.

"There are conditions to this arrangement," said Fred.

"Uh... okay."

"My business is my business and you need to keep your nose out of it."

"Okay."

"You and I will have no further contact. I don't know you and you don't know me." He pulled an extra key out of his pocket. "This is for the front door. I ever catch you in my stuff, the deal's off."

She nodded. He turned and waddled down the hallway, slamming and locking the back door as he left.

Eleanor dropped into a dining chair, stunned and confused. She studied her surroundings. Did Fred expect her to open a diner?

33

W**HITE PINE COUNTY** Sheriff Deputy Marty Prince sat at his desk contemplating the names of the recently arrested Hotel Nevada brawlers. Most were from a small town south of Twin Falls, Idaho. A wedding party gone wrong. A few locals. A couple from Georgia on a cross-country road trip. And a single guy from North Carolina. Joshua James Green. Probably a thousand of those out there, but something about the name rang a bell.

Marty looked through his wanted posters. Nope. Then he remembered a recent APB out of Montana. He flipped through the notices on his phone. There it was. Joshua James Green. Wanted out of Stone County, Montana for breaking and entering, attempted murder, and assault on a police officer. That one wasn't making bail. Attached to the APB, a BOLO for a guy going by the name of Richard Bale. Possibly an alias, and the description of his car.

Marty left the station and drove over to the Hotel Nevada. Unlike some local dive hotels, the Hotel Nevada co-operated fully with the police department. They ran a clean joint and wanted to keep it that way.

A tired, faded older woman manned the desk that night, probably past retirement age. More likely needing the job for extra cash than because she was bored at home.

Marty showed his ID and asked if a Joshua James Green was registered at the hotel. The woman flipped through the room registrations and confirmed. "Was he part of that brawl earlier?"

"He's sleeping it off. Did he come in with anybody?"

"Yeah. They checked in right after I came on shift. Him and another younger guy and a weaselly actin' older guy."

"Do you have their names?"

She studied the register. "Yeah. The other young guy is Logan Jones. The older guy paid for the rooms. Richard Bale."

"What did he list under vehicle?"

"White Mazda3." She wrote the license plate number on a sticky note, along with their room numbers. "You'll probably find the car in the side parking lot."

"The other two still in their rooms?"

"As far as I know."

"Thanks. I appreciate it." Marty walked out and around to the side lot. It was full of cars, most of them white, but only one Mazda and the plate matched the number on the sticky note. He called for backup and then went to his patrol car for a wheel lock. If the men tried to escape, it wouldn't be driving.

Groggy from sleep, Richard Bale considered ignoring the knock on his hotel room door. *Probably one of those dumb kids with something to complain about.*

The knock was persistent. And then came, "Sheriff's department. We know you're in there, Mr. Bale."

Richard's stomach clenched. He untangled himself from the sheet, jumped out of bed, and ran to the window. Third floor and no fire escape. *Pull yourself together.*

"We need to ask you a few questions, Mr. Bale. It would be better if you came out."

Richard took a deep breath. He felt cold sweat trickle down his back as he opened the door.

There was no routine questioning. After confirming their identities, Richard and a sleep-groggy Logan were taken into custody.

34

FRESH HOT COFFEE and a box of donuts greeted Peter and Helen as they dragged themselves into the sheriff's office on Monday morning.

"I heard you had a rough night," said Travis.

Helen groaned and grabbed a donut.

"How's our prisoner situation?" asked Peter.

"All five cowboys were bailed out as soon as they got here. There were some pretty upset wives. I'd hate to be those men this morning."

"And Phil?"

"Couldn't get ahold of his wife last night. He wasn't surprised. He said she'd take care of it this morning, but I called her and she said... and I quote, 'Let him rot in there!'"

"Did he get a lawyer?"

"Not yet."

"Who's on public defender duty these days?"

Travis turned to a laminated paper taped to the side of his file cabinet. It listed the public defender rotation for Stone County. "Ray Little."

"Give him a call."

Peter studied the box of donuts and picked a chocolate-frosted raspberry-filled. He broke off a piece and tossed it to Zack. "Angus in yet?"

"On a trespassing call. Out of state hunters on the wrong side of a fence."

Peter motioned everyone to follow him into his office. When they were settled, he turned to Helen. "So, what did you guys find yesterday?"

"A pool of dried blood hidden under a rug. Lots of blood. Luminol showed smears from the rug to the back door."

"From dragging a body?"

"That's my guess. There's also three sets of bloody footprints alongside the smear, two men's size ten and one size eleven. The size tens have different tread marks... different people."

"So, there were at least three men involved."

"Or large women."

"Does Eleanor have big feet?" asked Peter.

"Doubtful. She wasn't a big woman. Thank goodness we have good pictures of the prints. That group of goons trampling through things last night damaged evidence."

"One more thing to charge them with. How old is that blood, do ya' think?"

"No way to tell, really," said Helen. "Not unless it's still fresh and dripping."

"Anything else?"

"Nothing. Literally. Angus searched Eleanor's apartment. All the paperwork... business invoices... everything is under Fred's name. She doesn't even have a personal email."

"Weird."

"Yeah. We still don't know anything about her besides her first name."

"There must be someone in town who knows more about her. Doesn't she have friends?" asked Travis.

Peter thought for a moment and snapped his fingers. "Clem! She was at the Women's Club luncheon." He picked up his phone and scrolled through the contacts.

"She's upstairs in the forensics room," offered Travis. In the back corner of the outer office, wedged between the long worktable and eight-drawer antique oak file cabinet, a door led to a narrow set of stairs. The top of the stairway opened out into a large bright room filled with work counters and a variety of forensic equipment.

"What's she working on?" asked Peter.

"A new brand of superglue. She testing it out in the fingerprint fuming chamber." He turned and headed out the door. "I'll get her."

Peter listened to the clomp, clomp, clomp of Travis's boots going up the stairs and then the clomp, click, clomp, click of Travis following Clem back down. Clem, a longtime rancher's wife, insisted on spending her retirement dressed in skirts and heels unless winter weather forced her into slacks.

"Do you have a forensic projects for me?" she asked as she clicked into Peter's office.

"Not yet. Just a few questions."

That Clem did a poor job of concealing her disappointment was not lost on Peter. "What do you know about Eleanor?" he asked.

"Eleanor from the tea parlor?"

"Yeah."

Clem thought. And thought. "Nothing really."

"Her last name? Where she's from? Nothing?"

"Nothing. She's always the host. She never talks about herself."

"Does she have any close friends that you know of?"

Clem thought again. "No. I'm embarrassed to say, I go to the tea parlor and catered luncheons, but I don't think about her beyond that."

"She's like a ghost," mused Helen. "Everyone sees her but doesn't know who she is or why she's there."

"Angus packed everything from her office and brought it here," said Travis. "The desk computer and boxes of files from the filing cabinet."

"That's your assignment, Travis. Go through those boxes and see if you can find anything."

"On it, Boss." He left the room to begin investigating.

"What do you want me to do with the blood samples from the tea parlor?" asked Helen.

"Send a sample to the crime lab in Missoula. They can compare it to the Fred samples they have already. Since we don't have a body, is there anything in Eleanor's apartment or shop we could use to match her DNA to the blood?"

Helen and Clem glanced at each other.

"How about her toothbrush?" asked Helen.

"That would work," agreed Clem.

"Okay, Helen, go back and bag her toothbrush... and anything else you see that might be useful to the crime lab?"

"Got it."

Peter sighed. "So, if the blood is Eleanor's... and we presume she was murdered considering the amount of blood ... where is her body?"

"Should we check the landfill?" asked Helen.

"Couldn't hurt to look," said Peter. "Trailing her won't be much good from her shop. She would have gone in and out regularly, but I can use Zack at the landfill. When you're over there, grab a piece of clothing she would have worn recently."

"Will do."

They heard the phone on Travis's desk ring.

"Stone County Sheriff's Office... uh, huh... great... hold on."

Travis held the phone against his chest and grinned. "Sheriff's office in Ely, Nevada. They have Richard Bale and Joshua Green in custody... and another guy they were traveling with."

"Hallelujah!" said Peter. "Tell them we'll send someone to pick them up as soon as possible."

Travis relayed the message.

"How did they get them?" asked Helen.

"Drunk and disorderly."

"Not keeping a very low profile were they."

"Who are we going to send for transfer?" asked Travis.

"Call the transport service out of Missoula. We don't have the personnel to move three prisoners."

"On it, Boss."

Clem went back to her fuming chamber and Helen stood, yawned, and stretched.

"Grab that stuff from Eleanor's and then take the rest of the day off," said Peter.

"Thanks. I'm going straight to bed."

Peter put his feet on his desk, closed his eyes and thought. And slept.

35

BACK FROM HIS trespassing call, Angus studied the donut box on Travis's desk and grabbed a maple bar.

"Write any tickets?" asked Travis.

"No. They were decent enough guys. Rancher didn't want to press charges. Turned their map right-side-up and sent them on their way."

"Good." He brought Angus up to date on Richard Bale and Joshua Green.

"Do you have the Fred Filmore murder file handy?"

"Yeah," said Travis. He pointed to a file folder on his desk.

"Thanks." Angus picked up the file, poured a cup of hot coffee, and grabbed a second donut out of the box. He rolled a comfortable chair over to the work table and opened the murder file. Something had been niggling his brain. He needed to go back through the file. It was the pictures that caught his eye. Fred, lying on his back, front covered with diamond patterned lividity. He'd seen that pattern somewhere. He closed his eyes and mentally walked through the days since Wednesday when Nancy and her friends found Fred's body.

"That's it!" He slammed the file close. He hurried into Peter's office. "We need to get a warrant for Ernie Best's place."

"The guy who mows lawns?" asked Peter.

"Yeah." Angus opened the folder and showed Peter the pictures. "When I was there questioning him, I noticed this utility trailer parked by his lawn mower. He said he uses it to haul grass clippings."

"Okay."

"The metal bed of that trailer had this kind of diamond pattern."

Peter pondered. "Weak evidence for Judge Knowles to grant a warrant."

"He also had access to grass clippings and a blue plastic kiddie pool."

"Does he have any connection to Fred?"

"Not that I know of, but we don't know a lot of things going on with that Roost crowd. Besides, I just want to look at the trailer and compare it to the pictures. I'm not accusing Ernie of anything yet."

"Okay. It's worth a shot."

Peter called Judge Knowles who was in an agreeable mood.

He hurried through the usual preliminaries. "That sounds reasonable," said the judge. "But just the trailer. There's not enough evidence to search his house."

"Thanks, Judge. That's all we need." Peter disconnected and let Travis know to process the paperwork.

* * *

CURTAINS TWITCHED AND eyes followed Angus through the winding streets of The Burrow. He was relieved to find Ernie's house deserted and the basset hound secured in a nearby kennel. Howling protests he could handle as long as the howler and its teeth were in a cage. Ernie's lawn mower and trailer were parked under the carport. Not a mowing day.

Angus removed the pictures of Fred's body from the murder file on his passenger seat, took a good look around for possible hostile neighbors, and climbed out of his vehicle.

Under the carport, he compared the lividity pattern on Fred's body to the diamond pattern on the bed of Ernie's utility trailer. To Angus's eye, they were a match. Good enough. He backed his vehicle up to the carport, rolled the lawn mower out of the way, and hitched up the trailer. Before he left, he wrote a receipt and attached it to Ernie's door.

Eyes continued to watch as Angus drove back through The Burrow, but none tried to stop him. They didn't want that kind of trouble.

Back at the courthouse, Angus backed the trailer into an empty stall in the ambulance barn. He turned out the lights and closed the doors. Enough light seeped through cracks under the door that he could see to work. Peter and Travis came down from the sheriff's office and watched as Angus dug a spray bottle of luminol out of his crime scene kit. He sprayed a few squirts in the middle of the trailer. Nothing.

"Try one end or the other," said Peter. "He did most of his bleeding from his head."

Angus sprayed again, this time a sweeping arc across the entire trailer bed. Bingo. Smaller spots glowed here and there along the bed of the trailer, with a larger glob at the tail end. Travis hurried to take pictures while the glow was strong.

"What now?" asked Angus.

"We make sure it's human blood," said Peter.

"What else would it be?"

"If we asked Ernie why there's blood on his trailer, what do you think he would say?"

Angus thought for a moment. "Oh, it's hunting season. He would claim he was hauling a deer or elk carcass."

"Yep."

"How do we prove it's human?"

Travis grinned. "I'll go get the Hematrace™ kit." He flipped on the lights on his way out the door.

While they waited, Peter explained, "We swab the trailer on a spot that came up positive for blood and the Hematrace™ ABA card can tell us in about fifteen minutes whether we have a human or animal sample. We prove it's human and then we call Judge Knowles. That'll be enough evidence for an arrest warrant. Good job on connecting this trailer to Fred's body, Angus."

Travis came back with the kit, opened a swab, and sampled the area on the trailer bed where the most luminescence was seen. He placed the swab in a tube, added a buffer solution, and mixed it well.

"Now we let it sit for a few minutes," he said as he turned to the kit and took out a foil pouch.

He removed a plastic test card and dropper from the pouch. After a few minutes, he added four drops of the solution from the tube to the test card and noted the time on his watch.

"If we get two pink lines within ten minutes, we have human blood."

Angus, Travis, and Peter stared at the card, willing pink lines to form.

Travis began to smile. "See it?"

He passed the card to Peter, who grinned and passed it on to Angus. Peter took his phone out of his pocket and punched in the number for the judge.

HANKERIN' FOR FRESH trout and hearing good fishing reports, Ernie packed his fishing gear early Monday morning and headed for the Blackfoot River. What he didn't pack was his phone. He would have a good excuse when customers complained about not being able to reach him for last minute mowing jobs.

Later, standing in his driveway, full fishing creel in hand, he scowled at the empty spot under the car port. *Where's my dang trailer?*

His neighbors would have warned him if he'd had his phone. Leaving a message wasn't an option, easier to plead ignorance when crimes were involved.

That's where Peter and Angus found him. Ernie turned as the patrol vehicle pulled up to the curb. He made the connection in his mind. Trailer missing. The sheriff and a deputy. *They know.* His heart sank into his stomach and he swallowed vomit.

"Can I put my gear away?" he asked as Peter pulled out handcuffs and Angus read him his rights.

"We'll take care of it," said Angus, reaching for the creel and pole.

"That's full of fresh fish."

Angus hesitated.

"I don't care what you do with them," said Ernie. "Just don't leave them sitting in there to rot."

"We'll bring them to the jail," said Peter. "Maybe someone will fry them up for you... you're gonna' be there for a while."

36

"ACCORDING TO PHIL, he already confessed to stealing antiques from the Clara Hotel," said Ray Little, county attorney, sitting at Peter's desk with a cup of tea balanced on his knee.

"Yes, he did."

"And then he clammed up and asked for a lawyer?"

"Yep."

"I don't get it. What else do you suspect him of?"

"Murder."

"Is this about Fred?"

"Yep."

"I think you have the wrong guy."

"Of course, you do, you're his lawyer."

"He didn't say anything about murder when I talked to him. He's worried about theft charges."

Peter sipped his tea. "I think you're right. We have someone else who's a better fit for the murder."

"Where do we go from here?"

"Do whatever legal magic you have to do to get him out of here. We have three more guys coming in and I need the jail space."

"Are the owners of the Clara pressing charges?"

"Definitely."

"Who owns that place, anyway?"

"The owner prefers to stay anonymous."

"Weird. Anderson is a weird little town."

"I prefer *eccentric*."

Ray left and Peter finished his tea. He went to the jail cell holding Ernie Best. Ernie had not asked for a lawyer. He had not confessed to a crime. He had not denied a crime. He had not said a word after asking that his catch of trout be taken care of.

Peter unlocked the cell and pulled a folding chair in next to the bunk where Ernie lay on his back with his arm across his face.

"Ernie," said Peter.

Silence.

"We know the blood on your trailer is human."

Silence.

"How did human blood get on your trailer?"

Silence.

"Whose blood is it?"

Silence.

Peter stood and folded the chair. "We have a body. We have human blood on your trailer. You have access to the grass clippings and kiddie pool we found with Fred. If the lab calls and tells us that blood belongs to Fred, you're going down for his murder."

Silence.

Peter let himself out and locked the cell door.

"Hey, Travis."

"Yeah, Boss?"

"Where are the boots Ernie was wearing when he came in?"

Travis opened an evidence locker and handed over a pair of grass-stained Merrell hiking boots. Peter lifted the tongue of a boot. "Size ten."

Boots in hand, he two stepped up the back stairway to the forensic room where he found Clem bent over a work table, scribbling in a notebook.

"Hey, Clem, I have a project for you."

Clem sat up and smiled. "Finally!"

Peter handed her the boots. "Helen and Angus took pictures of three sets of bloody footprints at Eleanor's."

Clem pointed at the dark room. "I already have them developing."

"I suspect these boots will match one set of size ten prints."

He found a stool at another counter. "There's something else I wanted to talk to you about."

Clem looked worried. "Sure, Peter. Is there something wrong?"

"Um. Not really. This isn't about work... it's personal. A cold case."

Clem set the boots aside, full attention on Peter. "I'm intrigued."

Peter told Clem about the night long ago, his parent's final hugs as they left to celebrate a wedding anniversary in Missoula, and, later, the county sheriff's visit to break the news of their murder to Peter and his brother Paul.

"I'm so sorry, Peter. How old were you?"

"Eight. Paul was ten." His voice caught in his throat. "Their murder was never solved." He cleared his throat. "I have the murder file. I... I just can't bring myself to open it. To look at the pictures. I need someone capable, who I can trust. Would you work my parent's murder case for me, Clem?"

Clem grasped his hand. "I would be honored, Peter."

⁂

PETER FOUND HELEN dozing in his office when he came back downstairs. Two evidence bags sat on his desk, one holding a toothbrush and the other a brightly colored piece of clothing. Both were labeled with Eleanor's name.

Helen woke with a snort and wiped a bead of drool off her chin. "I found that blouse in her dirty clothes hamper so it should have a strong scent."

"Thanks. Now go home and get some sleep."

She yawned and stretched. "Gladly."

Peter grabbed the bags, lifted Zack's trailing harness and lead from its hook, and followed Helen out. He dropped the bag with the toothbrush onto Travis's desk. "Would you send that to the crime lab in Missoula? We need a DNA comparison with the blood from Ernie's trailer."

"Already have the paperwork filled out."

"Thanks. I'm going to the landfill."

"Looking for Eleanor's body?"

Peter shrugged. "May be a long shot, but I don't know where else to look."

Peter enjoyed his drive to the landfill. The vibrant green grasses and leaves of summer were quickly being replaced by gold and orange and burgundy. A cool nip in the air kept his windows closed, allowing the warm afternoon sun to cradle his face. He pulled into the landfill parking lot and was happy to see the mud of the week before had dried.

"Our days of hiking into the cabin are coming to an end," he said to Zack as he opened the kennel compartment.

Snowpack would quickly build on the mountain and block access until spring melt-off. Peter decided the brisk hour-long hike into his cozy mountain cabin would be a good way to clear his head and analyze the case.

"We'll go tonight... unless we find a body."

He fastened the trailing harness around Zack and clipped on the lead. After donning a pair of nitrile gloves, he pulled Eleanor's blouse out of the evidence bag and let Zack have a long thorough sniff. When he was finished, he looked at Peter expectantly.

Peter led him to where Fred's body was found. "Find," he said, and let Zack have his lead.

Zack showed no interest in the area. They walked from one end of the landfill to the other. Peter decided to walk around the fence and to the back. There, he gave Zack another good snuff at the blouse. They walked every trail and sniffed every pile. Nothing. Eleanor's body was not at the landfill.

As Peter loaded Zack into his kennel, he felt a hint of wet brush his cheek. Flakes of an early snow drifted in the air. He sighed. A hike to the cabin was out. They could be snowed in by morning.

37

Tromping around at the landfill in the cold left Peter with a sore throat and a foggy head. Hot tea with honey eased the pain, but he slept fitfully through the night. In the morning he made a house call to Dr. Hamm.

"It's probably just a cold," said Doc, as he looked down Peter's throat, and into his nose and ears. "Take it easy for the next couple of days. Plenty of rest, healthy food, lots of fluids. You know the drill."

"Hard to do in the middle of a murder investigation, Doc."

Lorene, the doctor's wife, set a steaming plate of Denver omelet smothered in salsa in front of Peter and another without salsa in a dish on the floor for Zack. She poured Peter a large glass of orange juice.

"There you go. Lots of protein and antioxidants."

"You're the best, Mrs. Hamm." He dug in and started chewing.

"Are you making any progress on the investigation?" asked Doc, as Lorene set an omelet in front of her husband.

"Baby steps. Hey, do you guys know anything about Eleanor from the tea parlor?"

"Eleanor? Sweet lady," said Lorene. "Do you think she had something to do with Fred's murder?"

"Not sure. She's missing and nobody knows anything about her."

"Gosh, I hope she's okay."

"You don't know her last name or where she came from? Where she would go?"

Lorene thought. "Ya' know. I went into the tea shop quite often, but she never talked about herself."

"How 'bout you, Doc?"

"I can tell you I never saw her as a patient. If she received medical care, she went out of town."

"Doesn't it seem strange to you that she lived here in the public eye for years and nobody knows anything about her?"

"Maybe, but some people like to keep to themselves."

"Speaking of reclusive people, do you have any updates on Mary?"

"I spoke with the hospital in Missoula this morning. She's still on the ventilator, but she's showing signs of coming around."

"Whew. That's great to hear."

Peter finished his breakfast, whistled to Zack, and headed over to visit his brother Paul's house. He planned to take a sick day without obviously taking a sick day. Let the public see him driving around town in his patrol vehicle while he hopped from one place of sympathy and comfort to another.

"You're sick," observed Linda when she opened the door.

Peter nodded. His throat had gone from sore to raw and his nose was completely clogged. He felt achy all over.

"Are you sure you don't have the flu?" asked Linda.

"Doc says it's just a cold."

"Well, get on in here and I'll make you a cup of hot tea." She ushered him into the living room. "Sit," she pointed him to a comfortable recliner. "Have you taken any cold medicine?"

"Not yet."

"I'll get you some." She left and came back with a soft fuzzy blanket, which she tucked around him, two gel capsules, and a cup of steaming Earl Grey.

As Peter sipped his tea and let the cold medicine do its magic, he asked, "Do you know Eleanor who runs the tea parlor?"

"Sure. I go in there now and then. She has a nice selection of used books."

"I mean, do you know anything about her? Like her last name? Where she's from?"

Linda hesitated. "No, but..." She settled onto the couch, ready to tell a story. "I met her the first day she came to Anderson. She was standing by the door of her building," Linda glanced at Peter, "before it was the tea shop."

"Wasn't it a lunch place before that?"

"Yeah. They called it The Coffee Corner, but they served sandwiches and stuff too. Some people from out of state owned it. The food was good, but they were only open a few months."

"And then Eleanor bought the place?" prompted Peter, knowing that Fred Filmore had actually owned the building.

"I guess. I was across the street at the bakery and saw her standing there. She looked so lost and alone and was obviously from out of town. I walked over and asked her if she needed help. She asked me where she could find a grocery store and I pointed her to Tom's place." Linda glanced again at Peter. "This is where it gets strange."

"How so?"

"She started walking to the store. I told her it was too far to walk and carry back groceries. She said she didn't have a car."

"How did she get to Anderson?"

Linda shrugged. "Good question. I guess she could have taken a bus. I gave her a ride to the store. While we were shopping, she said she wanted to open a diner, but didn't know how to cook."

"Did she mention where she came from or how she ended up in Anderson?"

"No. When I asked her questions, she was very evasive. In the end, she decided to open a tea parlor. I agreed to supply baked goods and she made simple sandwiches herself."

"But you never learned anything personal about her."

"Nothing."

As Peter contemplated Eleanor, his eyes grew heavy and he drifted off to sleep. Linda lifted the tea cup from his lap and tucked the blanket tighter around him. She went into the kitchen and phoned the sheriff's office.

"Stone County Sheriff's Office. Travis speaking."

"Hi, Travis. This is Linda Elliott."

"Oh, hi, Linda."

"Peter has a nasty cold. He's fast asleep in my living room and I plan on letting him sleep."

"So, don't bother him unless it's an emergency?"

"Exactly."

"Got it. Thanks for giving me a heads up."

Travis relayed Linda's message to the rest of the crew sitting around his desk sampling a box of specialty pastries brought in by Tom.

"Since the bakery's been out of business and Eleanor's Tea Parlor is closed," said Tom, "the grocery store is the only option in town for buying baked goods. These are samples from a new company. More expensive, but people will pay for quality."

Angus chose a chocolate croissant, took a bite, and chewed thoughtfully. "The bakery had nothing on this, Tom. It's great."

Helen and Travis quickly downed their own choices.

"I'd say three thumbs up," said Helen.

Tom smiled. "I'll put in an order today."

"Did Linda mention what Peter wanted us to do today?" asked Angus.

"No," said Travis, "but the transfer prisoners from Nevada should be here later this afternoon. They'll need processing."

"Any word on Birdie?" asked Helen, brushing crumbs from her shirt and ignoring the ones that fell through her gaping button holes.

"Doc said she's going to need at least a month for that wrist to heal." Travis took a sticky note off his computer screen and read, "He called it a 'taurus buckle fracture.' "

"The scientific name for Helen's back on night shift," said Helen. She grabbed an apple turnover as she left. "I'm going to bed."

"Can you do traffic duty?" Angus asked Tom. "I'll hang out here and wait for the Nevada transport. And cover any calls that come in."

"Sure. Peter has me scheduled until Birdie's back on her feet." He chose a blueberry scone before he stood and headed out the door "I didn't want to say anything to Helen until it's official, but Peter mentioned Birdie going to police academy when her wrist is healed. Helen will be on night shift for more than a month."

"She's not going to like that," said Angus. "Anything new in the murder department?"

Travis studied his notes. "Ernie Best has a short rap sheet. Mostly stuff he did when he was younger. Petty theft, that sort of thing."

"He lawyer up yet?"

"No, but refuses to talk."

"Nothing new on Eleanor or Fred?"

"Nothing. It's like they didn't exist before they came to Anderson."

"Maybe not their real names? How about this group we have coming from Nevada?"

Travis handed him a file folder. "The third guy is Logan Jones. He and Joshua Green have identical rap sheets. They've been hanging with each other for a long time."

Angus studied the file. "It says the younger guys drove a delivery truck."

"Yep. A judge in Ely signed a search warrant for both vehicles. The truck is full of antiques. The sheriff said we would have to send someone down for that stuff later, but everything else is boxed and on its way here with the prisoners.

"Good." Angus wandered over to the work table and studied the file while he waited.

38

I T WAS ELEANOR'S turn to panic. Everything she owned, including her nest egg of cash, was in her suitcase. And her suitcase was in Fred's van. Ignoring his warnings of staying out of the back, she ran to the door, flipped the lock, and flung it open. Her suitcase lay in the middle of the alley, unopened, where Fred had dumped it. She fell to the ground and cried with relief. Glancing up and down the alley to make sure he wasn't watching, she carried the case inside, locking the door behind her.

Suitcase stashed safely behind the counter, she began to explore. Pots, pans, dishes, and dinnerware filled cupboards and drawers. Bins of flour, sugar, and other staples lined pantry shelves. Eleanor didn't know the story, but apart from the layer of dust covering every surface, and an empty refrigerator, it looked like any other diner kitchen closed and ready for the next day's business.

In the other two rooms, she found an assortment of storage cabinets and display shelves. One cabinet was filled with neatly folded table clothes and cloth napkins in a variety of colors and patterns. Another held paper doilies and shelf liners. Cleaning supplies were stored in a small utility closet.

Eleanor knew how to set and clear tables, take and serve orders, and manage mealtime crowds. She could run a cash register and make change, but she had never cooked. Not even a little bit. How could she run a diner if she didn't know how to cook?

Continuing her exploration, Eleanor found a stairway that led to a small landing and a closed door. The door swung open easily, revealing a sunny living room. A kitchen opened on one side and a hallway on the other. The hallway led to a bathroom, bedroom, and office. Like the rooms below, the apartment, although covered with a layer of dust, was fully furnished. Was she supposed to live here?

Not used to being idle, Eleanor made her way down the stairs to the utility closet, gathered cleaning supplies, and started on the kitchen. While she washed away layers of dust, she thought about her options. On a back counter she found a familiar BUNN coffee brewer with three warming stations. Coffee. *I can make coffee... and tea.* But you can't run a diner with coffee and tea.

By midafternoon, the downstairs was dust free and Eleanor's stomach was growling. She found Saltine crackers in the cupboard, surprised they weren't out-dated or stale. Whoever had been running this diner hadn't been long gone.

Crackers temporarily eased the hunger pangs, but wouldn't get her through the night. She listened, hoping to hear Fred coming in the back door to take her to eat. She thought back on what he'd said, "I don't know you and you don't know me."

"He's not coming back," she said out loud. Now a middle-aged woman, she felt as vulnerable as that fifteen-year-old girl. No vehicle and no Fred. What she did have was money. If she was careful, enough to keep her going for a while.

Eleanor lugged her suitcase up the stairs to the apartment and took out a ziplock bag of carefully rubber-banded bundles of cash. She removed enough for a meal and stuffed the rest under the couch cushions. Not very original, but it would get her by until she thought of a better spot.

Outside on the sidewalk, Eleanor was at a loss to which direction to take. Once again a wave of loneliness engulfed her.

39

PETER WOKE WITH a start and sat for a moment getting his bearings. He recognized his brother's living room and could see the sun setting through a western-facing window. *Didn't I just eat breakfast?*

The room was empty besides himself and Zack, belly up, snoring on the couch.

Peter snapped the footrest on the recliner closed, stood, and wandered through the house. He found Linda in the study at her desk.

"Hey, sleepy head. How're you feeling?" she asked.

"Better," he croaked. "I need to get to work."

"No, you don't. I told them not to bother you unless it was an emergency." She shrugged. "So far no calls."

"So, you're saying I'm expendable?"

"At least for the day. Are you hungry?"

"Maybe a little, but my throat hurts too much to swallow."

"Get back in your chair. Another dose of cold medicine to cut the pain and a warm bowl of chicken noodle soup coming right up."

"What the doctor ordered?"

Linda laughed. "I did call and ask what you needed. He said rest and chicken soup."

Paul came in while Peter was eating. "Hiding from the public?" he asked.

"Mavis and the mayor, at least," croaked Peter. "You know how they are, me home sick during a murder investigation and they'll be calling for my resignation."

"We all saw you solve the last batch of murders."

"Pure luck and observant people helped solve those murders." Peter allowed a few bites of warm soup trickle down his throat. "By the way..."

"Yeah?"

He cleared his throat. "I asked Clem to work on Mom and Dad's murder case."

"Clementine Smith?"

"Yeah."

"Is she qualified?"

"Very much so. She has a degree in forensics. I'll request the murder box from Missoula. You okay with this?"

Paul nodded. "It's time."

Peter finished his soup and settled back in the recliner. His deputies could deal with murder for the day.

◆◆◆◆◆◆

"THEY'RE HERE," SAID Travis, setting down his telephone receiver.

Angus closed the file he had been studying, yawned, and stretched. "The cells ready?" he asked.

"Pillows are fluffed."

While Angus met the transport van in the back parking lot, Travis prepared for intake.

A mixture of demeanors walked through the door. Logan scared, Joshua sheepish, and Richard angry. None of them fought the cell. They were resigned to that. Travis took care of the necessary paperwork.

"Are you going to question them now or wait for Peter?" he asked Angus.

"Peter said to go ahead. Bring me the scared one first."

Travis checked his paperwork. "That would be Logan Jones. In Peter's office?"

"Yep," Angus flipped through the file cabinet and took out several *Waiver of Rights* forms, grabbed a pen and pad of paper, and made his way into Peter's office. He settled into the comfortable leather chair and took a deep breath.

Travis led Logan to a chair and handed his plastic bag of personal belongings to Angus.

"You are being charged with assault on a police officer, and attempted murder," said Angus. "Do you understand the charges against you?"

"Murder?! What?!"

"Those women you locked in that room almost died. One is in critical condition. If she dies the charge will be murder."

Logan sat silent. He had spent a few nights in jail in his time. He could handle that. What he feared was prison. The attempted murder charge was a shock. He made up his mind. Ratting out Josh, plea deals, whatever it took.

Exactly what Angus was counting on.

"Wait up, Travis. I need you to sign as witness." Angus began reciting from memory, "You have the right—"

"I don't need all that," interrupted Logan. "I know my rights. I don't want a lawyer. I'll tell you anything you need to know."

Angus suppressed a grin. "I appreciate that. You know how it is, though. If I don't follow the rules, my boss will have my hide. Hey, are you hungry?"

"Um... yeah, a little. We only had a sack lunch. That was a while ago."

"Let's get through this paperwork and Travis will bring you a good meal from the food truck. Pulled pork sandwich okay?"

"Gee, that would be great."

Angus finished reciting, allowing Logan to voice his understanding after each question. He flipped the rights waiver around so it was right-side-up for Logan.

Logan signed. Angus added his name and Travis signed as a witness.

Angus pulled Logan's wallet out of the property bag, removed his driver's license, and compared the photo to the man sitting in front of him and the signature to that on the form. Everything matched.

"Do you mind if I record this interview?" asked Angus after Travis left the room.

"Anything you need to do. Just get me out a' here."

Angus pulled a digital recorder from Peter's top drawer, set it on the desk, and pushed record. Anxious to please, Logan talked without needing to be questioned. He told about his younger years of petty theft and how he and Josh graduated to pilfering antiques and transporting them cross country. He told about meeting Fred and Fred leading them to Anderson.

Angus stopped the recording when Travis came in and set a to-go box in front of Logan. He added a pile of napkins and a set of plastic utensils. Angus watched Logan wolf down the meal, wash it down with a pop, and started the recorder again.

"Tell me about delivering goods to Anderson," he said.

"Same as always. We drove around the country looking for potential hits." More relaxed, he took a sip of his pop and leaned back in his chair. "You get to know what to look for. When the truck was full, we drove to Anderson, unloaded, and hit the road again."

"And Fred was always there to meet you?"

"Not always. If we were late coming in, he didn't like to get out of bed and drive into town. Especially in the winter. He gave us a key."

"I'm surprised he trusted you."

"He didn't. I mean, he said he had hidden cameras and he knew his inventory by heart. It was a good gig. We didn't dare mess it up by robbing him."

"What happened Friday night?"

"Richard was there waiting."

"Had you ever met Richard before that?"

"No. It was always just Fred."

"Did Richard tell you why Fred wasn't there that night?"

"All he said was Fred was gone and he was taking over." Logan hesitated. "The whole thing gave me the hibbie jibbies." Logan shrugged. "Richard offered to pay twice what Fred did and we had a truck full of stuff to unload. What the heck. Money's money."

"Did you go anywhere else in the building besides the hallway and store room while you were there?"

"Not usually. We did that night though. We went into that eating area."

"Why's that?"

"We were done unloading and wanted our pay. We went looking for Richard."

"Did you see anything unusual?"

"What do you mean?"

"When you went into the front part of the building?"

"Uh... no. Just tables and chairs and stuff."

"Everything seemed normal?"

"Uh... yeah." He looked at Angus. "Except Josh got in an argument with Richard."

"What about?"

"Josh thought there was something weird going on. He asked Richard about Fred again and said he was going to call him."

"How'd that go?"

"Richard got mad. Said he was the boss now and we had to deal with it. Then we heard those women talking in the back. Richard ran down the hall and slammed the door to the storage room and padlocked it." Logan took a long sip of his pop and squirmed in his chair, his knee jiggling. "We went outside and saw it was a sheriff deputy parked in back. We didn't want anything to do with lockin' up women, especially a sheriff deputy."

Angus stayed quiet for a moment, letting Logan collect his thoughts. "But you went along with it," he said.

Logan shrugged. "What could we do? We go to the cops and we get nabbed for all those stolen antiques. Besides, Richard's scary when he gets worked up. We thought he would turn us in if we didn't go along with him... or worse."

"Who dumped the patrol vehicle?"

"Josh drove. I followed and picked him up"

"Where was Richard at this point?"

"In town. He gave us directions to another shop. He had a load going to California. We filled the truck and headed out."

"And got as far as Ely, Nevada."

"Yeah." Logan hung his head. "Dang Josh. He just had to go partying."

Angus turned off the recorder and called Travis back in the room. "Mr. Jones is ready to go back to his cell."

"But I told you everything. Don't I get a plea deal or something?"

"Not in my power. That's up to the prosecutor. My advice to you is to talk to our public defender."

Logan slumped in his seat. "You can't put me back in there with Josh."

"We have a private cell downstairs."

ANGUS SAT STARING at the wall, deep in thought. He had two legitimate suspects in jail for Fred Fillmore's murder. He considered the possibility of Richard Bale and Ernie Best working together. *What would be their connection?*

"Travis?" he called into the outer office.

"Yeah?"

"Have we heard back from the crime lab about those blood samples?"

"Not yet, but I'll give them a call."

Several minutes later, Travis returned to Peter's office, notepad in hand, and sunk into a chair. "Initial testing has the blood type from Ernie's trailer, Eleanor's shop, and Fred all Type A positive."

"So, they could all be Fred's blood?"

"Not definite yet, but it narrows down the possibilities. Unfortunately, A positive is one of the most common types."

"So, the blood in the shop could still be from Eleanor?"

"Yeah. Or someone else. They have more testing they can do to narrow things down. Not having a blood sample from Eleanor or any of her relatives keeps us from knowing anything definite until DNA testing is done. That could take a while. The best they can do is determine whether or not the blood is likely Fred's."

"Not a lot of help at this point."

"The good news is Clem stopped on her way out. She said the tread on Ernie's boots match the prints in Eleanor's shop."

"Good. Okay. Let Ernie stew for a while longer. I want to interview Richard while that angle is fresh in my mind."

Travis led Richard into Peter's office and had him sit in the chair recently vacated by Logan Jones.

Angus informed Richard of his rights and that he was being held for attempted murder and assault on a police officer.

"What?" said Richard. "Murder? Assault? I didn't do any of that!" Richard's mouth hung open and he began to sweat.

Angus smiled. "I have witness testimony that you locked two women, including a sheriff's deputy, in an airtight room in the back of Eleanor's Tea Parlor."

"It wasn't me," yelled Richard, left eye twitching. "It was those two hooligans. They're trying to pin it on me."

"One of the women is in critical condition because of your action. If she dies, the charge will become murder."

"Can't I sign a statement saying it was really those other two guys?"

"First I have a few questions," said Angus. "What was your business with Fred Filmore?"

"I bought antiques from him."

"Were they stolen antiques?"

"I just bought them. I didn't ask where he got them."

In a flash of insight, Angus asked, "Did you use diversion tactics to lure unsuspecting ranchers away from their property so Fred could rob them?"

Silence.

"Did you murder Fred Filmore?"

"I want a lawyer."

Angus called Travis into the next room.

"Yeah?"

"Show Mr. Bale to his cell, please. Call in Ray Little. He wants an attorney."

Richard left the room fighting mad and cussing.

"Who do you want next?" asked Travis when he was finished with Richard.

"Bring in Ernie Best."

Travis brought in Ernie and had him sit in the chair.

"You are being held on suspicion of the murder of Fred Filmore," said Angus. He informed Ernie of his rights.

Silence.

Angus sighed. "Listen Ernie, the results came back from the crime lab. The blood we found on your utility trailer and the blood we found in Eleanor's shop match Fred's blood type. The tread on your boots matches the bloody footprints in Eleanor's shop. Whether you cooperate or not, you're going down for Fred's murder. We'll find Eleanor's body eventually, but, hey, you only need one murder conviction to get the death penalty. If you're lucky, you might get to spend the rest of your life in prison instead."

Ernie cleared his throat. "I'll tell you what happened."

40

"ELEANOR GREW UP on a ranch," explained Ernie. "She talked about her father, but never her mother. I had a feeling there wasn't a mom in the picture."

"Did she mention where the ranch was?" asked Angus. "Was it around here?"

"She never said," he glanced at Angus. "She was real skittish. It took a while before she invited me in for coffee. After I got through the door, I didn't want to push things."

Angus nodded in understanding. He had his own struggles gaining the attentions of a particular female.

"From what she said, her father wasn't the nicest guy in the world. She referred to him as 'my father', never dad. She said there were neighbor ladies who made sure she got to school, had decent clothes to wear, that sort of stuff. They would bring groceries by pretty regularly."

Angus bits the sides of his cheeks to keep from interrupting. He knew he needed to be patient and let the story come out.

Ernie coughed. "Could I have something to drink? All this talking is making me dry."

"Sure," Angus pushed the button on the intercom for Travis's desk. "Travis, could bring in some water for Ernie."

"Sure," said Travis. A few moments later, he came through the door and set a glass of water on the desk. "Anything else?"

"That's it. Thanks."

After Travis left, Ernie took a long drink and continued. "Eleanor said the ranch was a nice place, but her father was never satisfied. On the far edge of the property, just over the neighbor's fence, was a hay meadow with a spring-fed creek. He wanted that meadow. The old lady widow who owned it had sold off the rest of the property a little at a time but held onto that piece. She lived in a rundown farmhouse on the edge of the meadow. I guess she didn't want to break up the section."

Ernie took another drink. Angus stifled a sigh.

"After the old lady died, Eleanor's dad made a deal with the son. Her dad got the meadow and the son got Eleanor."

"What?!" said Angus in astonishment.

"Oh, not like what you would think. Like I said, the son was kind of a bum. His plan was to put Eleanor to work supporting him."

"How old was she?"

"Oh, about fourteen or fifteen, I reckon. They traveled far enough away from their home town that nobody would recognize them. He cut her hair and made her wear makeup so she'd look older. Passed her off as his little sister so nobody would wonder what he was doing traveling around with a young girl."

"What kind of work did she get at fourteen?"

"Waitressing. Bussing tables. Washing dishes. Any place they could find that didn't ask for ID and would pay under the table."

"How long did this go on?"

"Well, how old do you suppose she is now?"

"Fifties?"

"That's what I would guess. I never asked."

A lightbulb went off in Angus's brain. "Wait a minute. This guy... it... he was Fred?"

"Well, yeah. I thought you guys knew that."

⚬⚬⚬⚬⚬⚬

THROUGH THE YEARS they formed a sort of symbi-otic relationship. Eleanor briefly thought of running, but she had nowhere to go. No family other than her father. No friends. No money. No birth certificate or social security number or driver's license to find a legitimate job on her own, and no idea how to acquire those things. Truth be told, Fred didn't have those things either. They had each other and that was all. They lived on the fringes. Any hint of Eleanor making a friend or, even worse, garnering the attentions of a man, and Fred would pack them up in the night and move on.

FRED'S PLAN WAS for Eleanor to take the fall if the stolen antiques were ever discovered in the building in Anderson. He didn't expect her to open a tea parlor and become successful. From his recliner on the side-walk, Fred could see tables full of diners. He watched customers, shopping bags looped over their arms, cheerfully call out goodbyes as they exited the shop. Mostly, he heard the ka-ching of the cash register. Eleanor was making money and she owed him.

Late one afternoon, after the last of her customers left and Eleanor flipped the 'Open' sign to 'Closed', Fred used his key to enter through the back door of the shop. He made his way through the hallway, dropping his bulk into a chair at the edge of the dining area. The chair groaned, but held as Fred surveyed the room. His room.

Eleanor stifled a scream when she came out of the kitchen and found him there.

"What do you want?" she asked.

"You've done all right with this place while I've been busy with my antique business, but it's time for me to step in and manage things properly."

"What?!"

"I'll allow you to continue living in the apartment upstairs and you'll have a small allowance, but no more free rein with finances."

Eleanor clenched her fists as her blood pressure rose. "You said you wanted nothing to do with me. You said this was my area to do what I pleased."

"That was only while I got my antique business going. Things are running smoothly now and—"

Fred's final sound was a gurgle as the antique serving fork smashed into his skull and severed an artery. His great bulk slumped and then rolled onto the floor.

Blood flowed freely from the wound. The floor was well-built and level, which kept the blood in a neat puddle. Eleanor stood in shock. She stared at the handle of the fork protruding from Fred's temple.

Shock turned to panic. She needed help. She couldn't call the gentle ladies of the afternoon teas. She definitely couldn't call the sheriff. Then she thought of the man who came once a week on Monday mornings before the breakfast rush. Without being asked, he watered her hanging baskets and shined her windows. He would tap quietly at the front door when he was finished and they would sit over morning coffee. She told him of new recipes she wanted to try and he told her how pretty she looked in the morning sun.

Ernie Best was besotted with Eleanor. She had never called him, but she had his phone number on a piece of paper. "For emergencies," he said and she couldn't think of a greater emergency than the one that lay dead on her floor.

Ernie called two of his heftiest friends from the Roost. He attached his utility trailer to his truck. For camouflage, he threw in a load of grass clippings and a blue plastic kiddie pool salvaged from the recent wind storm.

The three men and Eleanor contemplated Fred's body.

"We need to get those clothes off him," said one.

"Why would we do that?" asked another.

"I was watching one of those CSI shows on TV. They took rug fibers and hair off the guy's clothes and figured out who killed him."

The others nodded. Eleanor found scissors and carefully cut away Fred's blood-sodden clothes. The men, with grunts and cussing, lifted Fred's body, lugged him down the hall and into the alley. They tossed him face down onto Ernie's trailer."

Eleanor brought the clothes, held out in front of her in disgust. "What are we going to do with these?"

"Toss them in the truck," said Ernie. "I'll burn them in my leaf pile."

"We can't drive him through town now," said one of the men. "Too many eyes."

"We'll wait until town's asleep for the night."

So, they covered Fred's body with a tarp, hoping the alley would stay quiet. Eleanor mopped the bloody hallway while Ernie and his buddies rearranged the furniture. The puddle of blood was too large for cleaning, so they covered it with a rug and topped that with a table. It made an awkward arrangement, but Eleanor didn't care. She wasn't going to stick around for comments.

In the wee hours of the morning, a heavy rain cleared the streets of any walkers, Ernie and his buddies drove to the landfill, dumped Fred's body, and covered it with grass clippings and a kiddie pool for good measure.

The next day, Eleanor closed her shop with the excuse of preparing for a catering job on Thursday. Fred's blood was beginning to smell and she couldn't open the shop knowing it was there. Thursday, she catered the Women's Club luncheon, learned Fred's body had been found, and began to panic.

She called Ernie. "I need to get out of here." She explained her problem. Nobody in town knew who she was or where she came from. They didn't know where she was going. Eleanor wasn't worried about fingerprints. There were no records on her. She worried about Fred and Fred's house and what the sheriff might find there.

"I'll take care of it," vowed Ernie, heady with visions of a knight rescuing a fair maiden.

"SO, YOU DUMPED Fred's body and then burned his house down," said Angus. "Do you have any witnesses to this?"

"The two guys who helped me move the body. They were there when she called."

"I need names."

"I can't rat out my friends."

"You can go to prison for murder."

Ernie hung his head and quietly recited two names.

"Okay, we'll bring them in. Last question. Where's Eleanor?"

"No idea."

"Do you want lethal injection or hanging?"

Ernie looked up un surprise. "They still hang people?"

"Oh, you're right. They did away with hanging. Lethal injection then."

"Eleanor murdered Fred. The guys will vouch for me. I don't know where Eleanor is."

"You said you would help her get out of town."

"I drove her to the bus station in Rumsey. It's a private company. They don't check IDs or ask questions as long as you have the cash to pay your fare."

"Where did she go from there?"

"Don't know. She wouldn't tell me."

"Did she tell you her last name? Where she was from?"

"No and no. I don't even know if Eleanor was her real name." He hung his head. "I feel like a chump."

41

MURDER DESTROYED MORE than a life in Stone County. It also smashed doors in Eleanor's mind she thought were sealed tight for eternity.

The best times were when he was busy. Early spring brought calving and planting. Later came branding and moving the herd into the hills to summer pasture. Cutting and baling hay, irrigating, and hauling water to the cows, these activities filled his days. He rose at dawn and collapsed into bed after a late supper, proud of the fact he did it all himself.

Winter brought a heavier darkness than what was caused by shortened daylight hours. Idle time laid bare his wretched soul. The alcohol he used to numb his brain only fueled the fury that spilled out in the dark of night. As she lay in bed, young Eleanor wrapped her pillow tightly around her ears to muffle noises coming through the thin wall between her bedroom and that of her parents. First would come the yelling, then the thump of fists against flesh. Screams turned to pleading and then muffled sobs. She was five when the bad thing happened, when she lost her mother. That night the screaming turned to silence, followed by a dragging and thumping down the narrow farmhouse stairs. She heard the front door hinges squeak and, eventually, the metallic ring of shovel against rock in the back yard. Eleanor slipped out of bed and crawled to the window, lifting herself enough for her eyes to breach the windowsill. Lying on the ground under an old oak tree was the still body of her mother, wrapped in her faded pink bathrobe. A pile of dirt grew next to the body as Eleanor's father dug and flung shovelfuls of dirt. As she watched, he lifted his eyes to her window, grinned, and cackled. Terrified, Eleanor crawled into her closet until hunger and a full bladder forced her out.

The house was never silent, but Eleanor knew the sounds of emptiness. The drip... drip... drip of a leaky faucet, the groaning of old wood, the slapping of a screen door left ajar. She crept down the stairs. Dusty moats filtered the bright morning sun. Through dirty windows she could see her father's combine chugging across a distant field. She was safe for a while.

Wanting to believe the night before was a bad dream, she made her way through the house and out the back door. She knew the truth of the horrors when she saw her beloved playhouse moved across the yard to cover her mother's grave under the oak tree.

Her father never physically abused her, but not out of any sort of decency. He was shrewd enough to know there were too many eyes watching. As far as he could tell, there were no suspicions about what really happened to his wife, but townsfolk weren't naïve enough to think he didn't beat her plenty before she disappeared. He didn't dare smack the kid around, but he could mess with her head. And he did.

He told the neighbors and townsfolk that her mother ran off with another man. Knowing of the abuse, it was an easy story to believe. The secret was safe with Eleanor. Every morning at breakfast, he would point his chin toward the grave under the oak tree and give her that evil grin. "There's plenty of room under there for you."

<hr>

A CHILL BREEZE blew through the valley, driving Eleanor toward the warmth of the house. She pulled her sweater closer as she let her gaze wander to the fence line. She took in the ruin of Fred's childhood home standing in the coveted meadow. The measure of her worth in her father's eyes and paid for many times over in her decades of service to Fred. She looked one last time at her mother's grave.

Justice rendered.

Thank you for
reading Justice Rendered!

Have you considered leaving
a review? Reviews help me
spread the word and help other
readers decide if they want
to enjoy the book, too.

Please scan the QR code
below and let me know
what you think! :)

-Kit

GET YOUR FREE EBOOK

Join the citizens of Anderson in *Mountain Tales,* an ever-growing collection of short stories about past and present mysteries.

SIGN UP AT KITKARSON.COM

BOOK 4 IS HERE

Holiday festivities in tiny Anderson, Montana take an unexpected turn when a welfare check becomes a murder investigation.

FIND IT AT KITKARSON.COM/BOOKS